The Other Side

A Novel

LILIYA GLAVATSKYY

The Other Side

For Beth Barnard —
awesome teacher
& person
♡

Liliya Glavatskyy

This novel is dedicated to my husband, Andrew Glavatskyy. He is the best husband any girl could ask for. I'm so blessed to have him in my life and always be by my side, ready to support me with all my ideas, sometimes even crazy ones!

Acknowledgments

The Other Side is my second novel. The idea came to me from nowhere. I was driving to work one winter morning, listening to music in my car, and observing the early morning, lonely streets. It was raining, like it always does in Washington State, and then I thought about snow.

Music and thoughts of snow floated through my mind…and all of a sudden, I had the plot for this novel. It was just the general idea, but as I started writing, the rest of it came to me in pieces.

Writing is my passion, so it wasn't hard to write this novel. In fact, I enjoyed every minute of it. However, I know that it wouldn't be possible without the support that I received from the following people; therefore, I want to offer my thanks to those who have helped and encouraged me during this process…

For Andrew, my husband: Thank you for always being there for me. I have known you for half of my life now, and we met when we were technically kids. So, when I talk about love in this novel, I know firsthand that true love is absolutely possible even at a very young age.

Thank you, Andrew, for helping to make me the person who I am today. Your love and support mean the world to me. Thank you also for reading each and every chapter of this novel when I was working on it. I loved hearing your feedback. And I love you more than you know!

For Jasmine Kovalevich, my niece: Thank you for being my biggest fan and for telling me how good the story was turning out. Thank you for taking the time to read every chapter of this novel and correcting many of the mistakes that I had made. Jasmine, you are the best! I love you and miss you every day!

For Valentina Tymoshchuk, my mom: Thank you for believing in me and helping me tremendously with my first book and for helping me financially with publishing my second novel. I love you and I miss you, mom! You're the best mom ever, and I hope you know that!

For Alla Sandu, my friend: Thank you, too—for reading this novel as I was still writing it; for reading it when it still hadn't been edited; for reading it when I was still in the process of figuring out the whole plot; for your feedback, which I value so much more than you can ever know! Thank you, Alla! You're a true friend, and I miss you a lot!

For Rebecca Denton, my nursing student and the editor of this book: Thank you for agreeing to work with me and for taking your time and effort to make this novel sound better than it sounded when I first finished writing it (and I do know that it was a lot of work!). Thank you, Rebecca! I'm so glad that we met!

I am a blessed person to have so many amazing people in my life! Thank you!

Part 1

One

Anna was quietly sitting at the table in the very far corner of the coffee shop. Nobody ever wanted to sit at that table, but she liked it. It was her spot. She felt almost invisible there. People came and left; they ordered their drinks, and they met their friends while she just sat and sipped her drink. Today, she was sipping green tea because she didn't have enough money to buy hot chocolate or a fancy coffee. Coming there wasn't about fancy drinks anyway. It was way more than that. It was about escaping her home life and spending some time in peace.

Anna looked at her backpack, old and worn out and not pink any longer like it used to be years ago; it was setting on the floor. She reached into the bag to retrieve her notebook and then opened it to the relevant page. It was getting late, and she needed to work on her homework. She would probably skip all the boring stuff and go straight to the chemistry, the only class she actually liked.

Anna liked chemistry for a few reasons. It wasn't hard for her, unlike her other classes. The teacher was the amazing, young and enthusiastic Ms. Emily. She never looked at Anna judgmentally, unlike other teachers did. Ms. Emily's lectures made sense, and she was fair when grading assignments. Also, Kevin was in the same chemistry class with Anna. And that was all it took, really. If Kevin was with Anna, she was happy.

After Anna finished working on her chemistry homework, she glanced at the clock. It was an old antique one on the wall of the coffee shop. Anna was surprised that it was almost ten o'clock. The coffee shop would be closing soon, and she needed to go home.

Home…what does home mean to other people? she thought.

Anna often liked to think about other people's lives. However, it usually made her feel very sad, so she would stop and occupy her mind with something else instead.

Anna checked her phone. It wasn't a fancy iPhone or Galaxy like most kids at school owned; instead it was an old scratched Nokia, but it worked so Anna couldn't complain. There was a text message from Kevin: *What r u up 2?*

There was nothing from her mom, no other text messages, no missed calls. Was her mom working late this evening? Or was she busy doing something else? Honestly, Anna didn't really want to know.

If it were up to Anna, she would just stay here, at the coffee shop, sipping her green tea and working on chemistry homework until it was time to go to school in the morning. But it wasn't up to her, and the coffee shop would be closing shortly. It was time to go.

Anna packed her things into her old backpack, put her Nokia into the back pocket of her jeans, and went to toss her paper cup.

"Are you leaving, Anna?" asked Robin, the only barista left in the coffee shop.

"I am. Have a good night, Robin," replied Anna.

"Have a good night. Coming again tomorrow?"

"I don't know yet. Maybe."

"See you then."

Anna went outside and immediately felt chilly, so she started walking quickly down the street. At that speed, she should be home in ten minutes.

Am I coming back tomorrow? Sweet Robin, she is always so kind to me. Even if I order just an iced water. She never makes me feel embarrassed, even though I am.

Oh well…as long as I don't have to spend the entire afternoon at home, especially if mom is there…especially if she has company. Mom…why can't she be normal?

Normal! Is that too much for a kid to ask for? Normal mom, even with no dad around. Clean home and clean clothes. Dinner. And at least a text message when her fifteen-year-old daughter is not home before midnight. I guess, it is too much to ask for…

Two

Anna opened the apartment's front door as quietly as she could. If she was lucky, her mom would already be asleep. And if she was, Anna surely didn't want to wake her mom up.

Anna didn't turn any lights on. Instead, she stood at the entrance for a few moments while waiting for her eyes to adjust to the darkness. And then Anna saw her mom. She was sleeping on the old, stained couch.

Her mom's hair was messy. Her left hand was still holding an almost empty wine bottle. Mom's hair used to be long and shiny, and Anna had admired her long black curls. But that was a very long time ago, in a previous life. Now mom's hair was faded and thin. It was always unevenly cut and, most of the time, it was pulled back in a ponytail.

Mom's hands used to be beautiful and warm—kind hands with brightly colored manicures and gorgeous rings. But that was in her previous life as well. Now mom's hands were skinny, even bony, and not gentle anymore. Also, nowadays she always had dark and chipped nail polish on.

Oh, Mama…

It was painful for Anna to see her mom like that. She still remembered and cherished the beautiful woman that she used to call "Mommy," but it seemed like that woman was a long time gone.

Will you ever come back to me?

With that question in her mind, Anna quietly went into the bedroom. It was the only bedroom in the apartment, and technically Anna shared it with her mom. In reality, it had been years since her mom had slept in the same room with Anna.

If Anna's mom was at home for the night, she would always sleep on the couch and not always alone. Anna stopped bothering trying to remember her mom's boyfriends' names as they seemed to change far too frequently.

Sometimes, her mom would go months without bringing anybody home, and sometimes she would even sober up enough to cook something nice for just the two of them. Anna loved days like that, but it seemed that with every year, those luxury days were becoming more and more infrequent.

Anna dropped her backpack on the floor and sat on her bed. The mattress squawked under Anna's weight and reminded her that she really needed to do laundry, including the linens currently on the bed, as it has been more than two months since she'd washed the sheets.

I'll do the laundry tomorrow. I just need to find some quarters. I'll check mama's wallet in the morning.

Then Anna pulled her old phone out from her pocket and plugged it in so that it could charge overnight. As she was undressing, she heard her phone vibrating. Anna picked it up and saw another text message from Kevin.

R u ok, Anny? Did u spend the whole afternoon @ the coffee shop again?

Anna frowned and typed a response. *If u know me so well, whyd u ask?*

Anny, dont be mad. Kevin's reply came instantly.

Im not mad!! Anna typed quickly.

Are u sure? U sound mad 2 me…

U cant hear how I sound right now. U r not here. Anna typed her reply and frowned again.

Im sorry I didnt spend the afternoon with u like I promised.

I dont care… Anyway, why didn't u? Anna felt snarkily satisfied in typing her response.

It was Lauren. She had another episode. my mom had 2 work n I had 2 watch her.

Anna felt embarrassed and guilty. Sometimes she acted like a selfish child, but she wasn't a child anymore. She needed to grow up.

Lauren was Kevin's younger sister. She had lots of health issues, including epilepsy. Lauren was a sweet little girl who was very happy about absolutely everything in the world despite being sick most of the time. Anna envied that.

Anna herself wasn't as happy as Lauren was. Anna always wanted more from her life. She wasn't happy with her home life; she wasn't happy with her school life. Sometimes she even suspected that she was truly depressed, but who was she to know what true depression looked like? It's not like she had a mom who cared enough to notice something like that and take her to the doctor.

Anna hadn't seen her pediatrician in years. When Anna felt sick, she just found some Tylenol and stayed at home for a few days until she felt better again. Then she wrote herself a note and signed her mom's signature so that she could return to school. That was Anna's life…

Kevin Im sorry. Hows Lauren now? Anna sent her response.

Dont be sorry, it's ok. Laurens better. She was really tired all evening n now shes sleeping. Im watching her until moms back. I dont want 2 leave her alone.

U r such a good big brother. I hope u know that. What about Kate? She home?

Kate was Kevin's older sister; she was the oldest of the three siblings. Actually, Kate was only a half-sister to both Kevin and Lauren, and she acted like only a "half-sister" if anyone would ask Anna for her opinion. Kate was selfish and cared only about herself. It seemed like nobody else noticed that though, and it was only Anna who felt that way.

Kate had plans so she left. Anna read Kevin's response.

She working? typed Anna.

I dont think so.

I see… Just as Anna had suspected. Smiling ironically, she sent her response.

Anny, leave her alone. Kates not that bad. She helps when she can.

U r right…

Oh well… I don't think you 2 will ever like each other.

I'll like her if she changes n acts adult! Anna felt angry again as she typed her response.

Then Anna thought about her own mom who didn't act like an adult, but Kevin never judged her mom's behavior or life choices. He never made any negative comments. He never made Anna feel embarrassed because of how her mom was.

Anna felt guilty again. *Why do I do this? Why am I so bitter?*

Kevin, its not my day 2day. Please ignore every bad comment I made. I'll be better tomorrow. I promise. Have a good night. See u @ school tomorrow.

See u tomorrow. Love u. Anna read Kevin's text message and smiled.

Love u 2.

Anna laid down and closed her eyes. She thought about Kevin for a moment more. She was so grateful that he was in her life. She needed to start treating him better. She was not being fair with him, especially lately.

Kevin was such a nice guy—an amazing son and brother for his family, good at school, and he planned to start working in a few months when he turned sixteen to help his mom with the bills. Anna admired Kevin as a person, and she loved him with all her heart.

Then why am I so negative with him sometimes? Especially when he didn't deserve that? Anna didn't have any good answers to her own questions.

Three

The next day Anna woke up and immediately went to the living room to check if her mom was still there. She was gone. There was no note on the fridge saying "I love you" or "See you tonight." There was no breakfast on the table. There was just a lonely, empty wine bottle next to the couch where her mom had slept last night.

The usual... pondered Anna as she opened the pantry door and reached for an almost empty cereal box. She poured some cereal into a bowl and opened the fridge to get some milk, but there was no milk. Anna forgot until that moment that she had finished the last few ounces the day before.

Dry cereal it is! Anna thought to herself.

She sat down and quickly ate. Then she went to scrounge some cash. Anna looked under the couch; she checked her mom's pockets, and she checked a shoebox that was hidden in their bedroom. She found nothing.

Man, I really need some cash. We need food. Maybe mama will buy something today, but I also need to do the laundry. And I'm not even thinking about the coffee shop right now.

Anna kept searching the apartment because she knew from past experience that she might be able find cash in random places.

She'd found a few dollars in the door next to the utensils last month, and once she'd found a whole twenty dollar bill in one of her mom's shoes. Anna didn't know if mama hid the money on purpose or if she was too drunk to think clearly. To be honest, Anna didn't really care. As long as Anna had some money to buy food and go the coffee shop, she was satisfied.

It was Anna's lucky day. She found one dollar bill and seven quarters in a little vase in the bathroom.

Well, it's better than nothing.

On her way to school, Anna was thinking about her plans for the day. There wasn't much she could really plan, but thinking about such things made her feel better, like she was in control of her own life. Like there was something she could control. Like she had a life!

Christmas was coming up. Everyone around Anna was preoccupied with the topic. Questions like "Are you ready for Christmas?" or "Have you finished your Christmas shopping yet?" were everywhere, and these questions drove her nuts.

No, she wasn't ready for Christmas! Moreover, she didn't care about Christmas! *What's so special about it anyway? Families getting together and giving each other presents?* Well, she didn't have that kind of life, so she couldn't care less.

But deep in her heart, Anna envied people who talked happily about Christmas and buying presents, going to church, baking cookies, and all that...stuff.

Deep in her heart, Anna wanted what others had. She only remembered one happy Christmas. She'd had it with her mom when she was four or five.

Deep in her heart, Anna hoped that one day she would be one of those people talking happily about holidays coming up and making plans. But for now it wasn't her life.

Anna's life was sad and lonely. It was only Kevin who kept her going. If it wasn't for him, Anna wouldn't be here. She knew that for sure.

Thoughts about Christmas and Kevin reminded her that she didn't have a present for him. He would be the only person that she would have loved to give a present to, but where should she find money for that? Anna felt helpless. She wasn't old enough to work and that was a major issue because she would do any kind of job in a heartbeat.

Then Anna thought of something that made her feel instantly guilty. *No, I won't do that. No, no, no.*

Anna had promised herself the last time that she wouldn't do it again. But then she had promised herself the same thing several times in the past. But...she kept doing it anyway. Anna knew that stealing was absolutely wrong, and she could get in a lot of trouble if caught. She wasn't stupid! But she was desperate. And when she was desperate enough, she didn't think clearly.

Christmas was in three days, and she needed to figure something out today or tomorrow so that she would have a present for Kevin. She loved him enough to steal for him.

But that's so wrong! Isn't it? Well... I don't care. I just don't care right now! I will do it this last time. I promise. Just this last time and then next year, I'll be old enough to hold a job, and my life'll be different. It will be very different.

Four

After school, Kevin wanted to hang out with Anna. But Anna said that she had lots of homework to do, and she had promised her mom to do the laundry. Kevin hardly believed Anna, especially about the homework. It was the last day of school before the Christmas break, and Anna never really cared about school stuff anyway. Still, Kevin knew very well that it was pointless to attempt stopping Anna from whatever she had in her head. She was stubborn like that. And, for some reason, this stubbornness attracted Kevin. So, he simply kissed Anna goodbye.

"I'll text you tonight, Anny," he said.

"Okay."

"Any plans Christmas Eve?" asked Kevin.

"You're kidding me, right?!" Pretending it was funny, Anna offered these words with a light tone and forced a laugh, but her young and immature soul was crying inside. She wished with all her heart to have special plans this Christmas Eve. Plans that would involve her family, her mama…

"Well…I was just asking."

"What about you? Do you have any plans?" asked Anna.

"Not really. Mom's working Christmas evening and the whole night, actually. She always works on holidays. The pay's too good not to. Kate'll be out somewhere. So, I'll need to keep an eye on Lauren. Do you wanna come over?"

"No, I think I'll just stay home. Can you meet me in the coffee shop in the afternoon? Before it gets too late, and they close? I'm sure they'll be closing early on Christmas Eve."

"You're sure you don't wanna come over?" repeated Kevin.

Anna just stared at him and, once again, he knew that he wouldn't be able to change her mind.

"Okay, Anny. The coffee shop it is. I'll see you there."

He kissed Anna again. She seemed in a hurry, though. She quickly pulled back, turned around, and started walking away from him. She had a mission to accomplish.

As Anna was walking, she was thinking intensively. Where should she go? Her first idea was Walmart, but no, she wasn't stupid like that. She knew that people tried to steal from Walmart and got caught all the time. No, she needed something different.

Also, she didn't need a small store with just a very few customers and workers staring at her; no, she needed something different.

Anna kept walking and thinking. Suddenly, she had an idea where she should go to get a present for Kevin. She should go to a store where it's busy enough but where people didn't usually steal and no one would suspect her. Anna was almost proud of herself.

Soon, Anna reached her destination. She felt anxious and scared. But she had made her decision, and nothing was going to change her mind. Thirty minutes later, Anna felt exhausted. She needed to hurry up and just do it. But it was harder than she had thought.

Anna really liked a pair of Nike sneakers, and she knew that Kevin would be beyond excited to own a pair of shoes like these ones, but she didn't have the nerve to just grab a pair of sneakers and run. No, she needed something else.

Anna spent some time looking at colognes. There were a few she absolutely loved.

Just imagine, Kevin's kiss on my lips, and he smells like this...

But that gift wasn't possible either. Only the opened bottles were displayed out on the table, and most of them were half or almost empty. Anna wasn't pathetic enough to give Kevin one of *those* as a Christmas gift. In any case, Anna would have to ask one of the workers for a new cologne bottle and that would be it—she would need to pay for it right away. Anna gave up this idea and went to look at other options.

Glass tables displaying jewelry caught Anna's eye, so she went in that direction. She skipped all the displays with women's jewelry. She wasn't here just to steal; she had a bigger goal—Kevin's Christmas present. So, Anna went to the display that had men's jewelry.

There were rings that Anna really liked, but she didn't know Kevin's size. There were watches, but they were too expensive, and Anna didn't think they were right. And then she saw a few bracelets.

Anna picked up a few of them and checked the prices. She liked one bracelet in particular; it was made from leather, and it wasn't too expensive. Anna looked it over one more time, and then she glanced furtively around. No one was looking at her.

Anna looked again, just to be certain. The only worker who was in the jewelry department was assisting a female customer. The customer was laughing loudly as she took out her wallet to pay. The woman's wallet was thick, and it was made from bright red leather.

Anna stared at that woman customer and her wallet while Anna's own hand quietly slipped into her coat pocket. And in it, she was still clutching the bracelet. Just a moment later, Anna was leaving Nordstrom.

No one was following Anna. No one was running after her. But Anna felt like everyone around her must know. They all saw, and they all knew what kind of person she was…but it didn't matter because it was the last time. She promised herself that this time would be the very last time.

Five

It was Christmas Eve, but Anna couldn't feel worse. She wanted to give her present to Kevin, but every time she thought about the stolen bracelet she felt disgusted with herself.

What kind of person am I? I'm so pathetic...

Anna hadn't seen her mom for the past two days, and she was starting to worry about her. Usually her mom would still come home even if she was in no condition to do or say anything. Anna just hoped that her mom was working extra shifts like Kevin's mom, Elizabeth, was. But her own mom was so very different from Elizabeth.

Elizabeth lived for her children; they meant the world to her. She was a hardworking and caring mom. Elizabeth was slightly overweight, had a soft voice and a soft temperament. Anna never saw Elizabeth drunk or mad; Anna didn't think it was even possible.

Elizabeth had been happily married to the same man for many years, but he passed away three years ago from a brain tumor. Elizabeth had been devastated, but the tragedy didn't break her. After her husband's death, Elizabeth started working even more, but she still managed to fully focus on her children. She didn't date anybody, probably because she simply didn't have time for that between two jobs and three children.

Anna's mom was a different story… She had been "normal" once, but that was a long time ago. She changed her jobs and her boyfriends way too frequently. She hadn't talked to her own parents, Anna's maternal grandparents, for many years, so Anna didn't even know them. They lived in a different state.

Anna's mom was very skinny, almost anorexic-looking, and she wasn't gentle and caring anymore.

Anna was still thinking about her mom when she felt her phone vibrate. She picked it up and saw a text message from Kevin.

Hey Anny, how r u? running late, srry. Will meet u @ coffee shop but not @ 4, maybe more like 430 ok?

Anna felt immediately irritated. She was very anxious and wanted to see Kevin as soon as possible. He had a calming effect on her. She always felt really good being with him.

Anna texted him back. *Ok. But please hurry. They close @ 7 2nite.*

Ok, will be there asap, C u soon. His reply came instantly.

Anna decided that she couldn't stay home any longer. She felt claustrophobic there. She wanted to go out and be around people, even if they were strangers to her.

To get herself ready, Anna first pulled on a pair of old and faded jeans and her favorite oversized gray sweater. Then she ran her fingers through her short brown hair and looked in the mirror. Lastly, she added some mascara and eyeshadow, which she thought made her look older. Another glance in the mirror and she felt satisfied.

Anna put on her coat and boots and went outside. She started walking down the street toward the coffee shop. However, she soon realized that it was very cold outside, so she sped up.

In less than ten minutes, Anna was entering her favorite coffee shop, wishing for only one thing in that moment—to have a few dollars in her pocket to buy a hot chocolate. Iced water didn't sound appealing at all when she was freezing.

Oh well, I'm used to it anyway…

"Anna! What a surprise to see you this evening! You're not at home for Christmas Eve?"

It was the sweetest barista in the shop, Robin, talking to her. Robin always called Anna by her name. In fact, Robin was actually the only one here who did that.

"Hi, Robin. Um…no, I just wanted to go for a walk. And I am meeting Kevin here pretty soon."

"Oh, okay. Would you like something to drink, sweetie?"

"Yeah, can I have an iced water, please?" Anna's face flushed when she voiced the words. She could feel her cheeks turning red and hot; she felt so embarrassed.

"Sure. I'll bring it to your table in a minute, Anna," said Robin.

"It's okay. I can wait here."

"I actually need to do something really fast, and then I'll get you your water. Is that okay?" asked Robin.

"Sure. Thank you."

Anna calmed down. Robin was such a nice person. She wasn't judging Anna. Anna was sure of that.

Anna took her coat off, as it was very warm and cozy in the coffee shop, and went to sit at her favorite table in the dark corner. Then she looked at the clock; it was almost four o'clock. Kevin should be there soon.

"Here is your drink, honey. Iced water as you asked, and here's a tall hot chocolate with extra whip cream!" Robin's voice was cheerful.

"Um…I didn't ask for the hot chocolate. Sorry."

"I know you didn't. The cocoa's on me tonight, sweetie. Merry Christmas!"

Anna looked at Robin, and she felt tears welling up in her eyes.

"Thank you, Robin. Merry Christmas to you, too."

Robin set Anna's drinks down on the table, turned around, and quickly disappeared. Anna tried her hot chocolate, and it tasted so good. It was the best hot chocolate she'd ever had.

Six

Anna quietly sat in her dark corner and slowly sipped on the hot chocolate with the extra whip cream. There were no other visitors at the coffee shop besides her. Robin had disappeared behind the small door that was located behind the counter, and suddenly Anna felt like it was just her in the entire whole world.

No wonder Anna felt as she did: It was Christmas Eve after all. It was getting dark outside, and even the street outside looked very lonely.

Everyone else is probably at home celebrating with their families...

Anna looked at the big antique clock on the wall and noticed that it was almost five o'clock. Kevin hadn't come yet.

At first, Anna wanted to get mad at him, but then she decided that it wasn't an evening to get mad at people. Robin was so nice to her, and she should be just as nice to Kevin in return. Anna wasn't sure if things really worked like that, but she wanted to believe it.

As the minutes passed by, Anna felt sadder and sadder. She really wanted to be with Kevin. She didn't know what was taking him so long, but she didn't want to text him either. Knowing herself, she'd probably get mad right away, and she didn't want to.

Anna looked through the window again and couldn't believe what she saw—it was snowing. Delicate snowflakes were falling down, and the snow looked so beautiful. She couldn't remember the last time it had snowed, maybe two or three years ago, and now it was snowing on Christmas Eve.

White Christmas. Magical Christmas… thought Anna to herself. She grabbed her coat to go out and look.

Once outside, Anna simply stood by the entrance and stared. She couldn't believe how beautiful and magical everything was beginning to look, coated in a white frosting of snow. Anna felt so peaceful. However, she got very cold in just a few minutes and decided to go back in to text Kevin.

When Anna went back inside, she noticed people were sitting at the table on the other side of the coffee shop. It took her off-guard because she hadn't noticed anybody come in. She stared for a second, shook her head, and walked back to her table.

She took her cell phone out, but the sudden appearance of those customers just bugged her. *How did I not see them coming in? How did I not hear them ordering their drinks? Robin is so loud and cheerful that it's impossible not to hear her.*

Anna felt so curious about these people that she found herself wanting to stare. One was a teenage girl, probably Anna's own age or thereabouts, and the girl was sitting facing Anna. The other person seemed older, but Anna could only see the back of her long dark hair and her bright coat. The two were talking cheerfully, and the teenage girl was smiling at her companion.

Anna didn't want to be rude or apparent, so she tried not to glance for longer than a few seconds a time. She looked at her cell phone again and remembered to text Kevin this time.

Hey, u still coming? I'm waiting 4 u. Everything ok?

Then Anna looked back to the customers across the coffee shop. The girl was saying something and holding her drink like she wanted to drink whatever it was that she had in the cup, but she was too busy with her story.

Then Anna heard the other person laugh, and it gave Anna chills. She knew that laugh! She definitely knew that laugh! Anna felt like time had stopped. She was shocked.

But then Anna's phone vibrated in her hand, bringing her back to reality. She looked down at the screen. It was a text message from Kevin.

Srry, Anny! running late. Will b there soon. C u in 5. Will explain when I get there. Please dont b mad.

Anna wasn't mad. Anna was still in shock. She looked at the coffee shop visitors again. This time she stared at the girl whose face she could see and actually paid attention to it. The girl wasn't looking at her, so Anna didn't worry about being rude. Actually, she didn't care at this moment.

Oh my goodness, this just can't be true…No, no, no, this can't be happening. Am I losing my mind? Am I psycho or something? Wait, where are they going? Are they leaving already?

The other girl stood up and so did the other person. Then the one who'd been facing away turned around, and Anna froze. She was looking at her mom. But a different version of her mom. The woman looked healthy and beautiful. In fact, she looked stunning, dressed in nice jeans and black sweater with a hot pink coat with fur on top. She was putting her expensive-looking purse on her shoulder, and then she looked at the girl and smiled at her.

"Let's go?" Anna heard her mom saying.

"Yeah, let's go. We still have lots to do at home." It was the girl responding now.

Even more shocking was looking at the girl. By now Anna was overtly staring at both of them. She saw her mom, and she saw herself. It was her, Anna, or rather another version of Anna standing just fifty feet away from her. The two got their stuff and quickly walked toward the front door.

It took Anna a second, but then she jumped from the seat and went outside, following the two. She didn't know what she was doing or why she was doing it, but the impulse was strong.

However, when Anna opened the door and looked outside, there was nobody there. She stood for a minute looking in different directions, but she saw no people on the street at all. She took a few steps away from the coffee shop entrance and kept looking, but again, she saw nobody.

About five minutes later, more anxious than ever, Anna came to her senses.

What in the world was that? What in the hell just happened here?

At least now Anna was able to begin thinking again and process some thoughts in her head even though she still felt completely confused. Then she felt the freezing chill outside. She decided to go back in and was surprised once again.

There was Kevin sitting at the table, waving at her.

"Anny! Where have you been?! I've been waiting for you for a while, and Robin said she didn't know where you went."

"Wait. What? You texted me just a few minutes ago saying that you're on your way."

"That was over half an hour ago," said Kevin.

"Are you serious? Don't blame me when you're the one being late!"

"Anny, you're too funny. Check your phone."

Anna looked at Kevin in disbelief, and then she checked her phone. There it was—Kevin's text message, received at 5:01 p.m. Then Anna looked at the clock and realized that it was almost six now.

"But *how*?"

"How what?"

"Nothing...It's nothing. Never mind me. I just got bored sitting here all alone."

"Where'd you go?"

"I went outside to see the snow. It looked so beautiful."

"Did you go far away?" asked Kevin.

"No, I was just right there by the entrance."

"Oh, that's weird. I didn't see you when I came in."

Anna didn't know what to say. She felt her head was a jumbled mess, and she needed time to sort everything out. She leaned closer to Kevin and hugged him.

"I missed you so much. I'm glad you came."

Kevin hugged her back tightly and whispered in her ear, "I love you, Anny."

They sat down, but then Kevin promptly got up and went to order chocolate chip cookies for both of them and one hot tea to share.

Within a few minutes, Anna was chewing her cookie and listening to Kevin with half an ear. His story was interesting, but her mind kept wandering a hundreds miles away. She was thinking about that teenage girl and that woman who definitely was her mom...but not.

"Anna?" asked Kevin.

"Yes?"

"Are you listening to me?"

"Yes, of course I am!" she replied although she had no idea what Kevin had been saying a second ago.

"Do you wanna know what that is?" asked Kevin.

"What is what?"

"Your Christmas present!"

"Oh! You got me one?!" Anna was so surprised.

"Yes! That's what I was saying!"

"Yes, yes, I heard you. Of course, I wanna know what it is!" Anna smiled at him.

Kevin reached in his coat's inner pocket and retrieved a small blue paper bag. He gave it to her and quickly said, "I hope you like it."

Anna opened the bag and looked inside. There was a small, cute mirror. It was square, light pink in color, and there was a drawing of a girl with the words, "hello, gorgeous" next to the female figure.

"Oh, thank you, Kevin. It's so adorable! I love it! It's something I'll use every day. This is so nice of you!"

Anna leaned across the table and gently kissed Kevin. He blushed. He always did whenever she kissed him. Then she put her hand in her pocket and pulled the bracelet out. She put it on the table in front of Kevin and simply said, "Merry Christmas!"

Kevin looked surprised, but he didn't ask any questions. He knew that she found cash from time to time at home, and the bracelet didn't appear too expensive anyway. Kevin put the bracelet on and smiled at her.

"I really like it. I'm going to wear it all the time, so it can remind me of you."

Anna started laughing.

"So, you need to be reminded about me?"

"You know what I mean!"

Yes, Anna knew what Kevin meant. She was just teasing him, but she still felt guilty looking at the bracelet. However, she also had so much on her mind in that moment that it was easy to put how she'd gotten the gift into the back of her mind.

Kevin had moved onto telling her a new story, and she pretended she was listening, throwing a quick "wow" and an "uh-hum" here and there. In reality, though, Anna's mind was far away. It was chasing the mysterious teenage girl and the lady who was Anna's mom. Or looked like her mom anyway...

Seven

Anna woke up on Christmas Day to the delicious smell of coffee. She felt confused for a second.

Where am I? What's that smell?

Anna wasn't used to breakfast smells. Not anymore. The aromas of coffee, bacon, and eggs in the apartment didn't feel right anymore. They jarred her senses. Anna felt like it had been ages since anything normal and nice had happened in her life.

Curious and uneasy, Anna got up and went to the kitchen. She couldn't believe her eyes. Her mom was standing in front of the stove making an omelet. She heard Anna coming, so she turned around and smiled at her.

"Hey, Anny. Merry Christmas! Are you hungry?"

Anna was quiet for a second. She didn't know what to say. A flood of emotional thoughts ran through her brain. Anna wanted to ask her mom where she has been for the last two days and why she was in such good mood all of a sudden. She wanted to tell her mom that she really needed some cash, and the laundry still needed to be done. Anna wanted to tell her mom about the coffee shop mystery last evening, and she wanted to ask her mom if that had been her. There was so much that she wanted to ask and to tell her mom. She felt overwhelmed. So, instead Anna simply smiled and sat herself down at the kitchen table.

"Coffee? Or hot chocolate?"

"I'll have some coffee with you. Thanks."

"Cream and sugar?"

"We have cream?" Anna was surprised.

"We do. Hazelnut. I hope you like it."

"Okay!"

A plate with an omelet and bacon appeared in front of Anna, and she stared at it for a second. Then a cup of steaming coffee joined the plate right in front of her. Anna was still looking down at her food when her mom started talking again.

"Aren't you hungry?"

"What? Um, yes, yes. I am actually."

Anna started eating her food, and it was just delicious. It was the best breakfast she had eaten in months. Or maybe years? It didn't matter. She was too afraid to ruin the moment. So, she ate and sipped on her coffee with the hazelnut creamer in it, pretending like eating a meal with her mom was a normal thing to do, like it was something casual in her life.

Her mom was eating next to Anna, but they both were quiet. It was almost awkward, but then her mom got up and went to the sink to wash her dishes.

"Are you done? Can I have your plate?"

"Yes. Thanks for the breakfast. It was really good."

"You're welcome, honey. When does school start again?" asked Anna's mom.

"Um…in a week or so. Why?"

"Nothing. Just asking."

Anna stood in the kitchen for a moment not knowing what to do or what to say. There was so much Anna wanted to say, but she felt like she had forgotten how to talk to her mom. Seeing the woman acting like this was so strange, not to mention her carrying on a clear, normal conversation.

"Okay, honey, it's time for me to go. I'll see you tonight."

Honey?

"You're leaving already?" Anna was surprised. And disappointed.

"Sorry. My shift starts in thirty minutes. I don't wanna be late to my new job. It's a good one, and I really like it so far. I'll tell you more about it when I get back."

"Okay."

Anna's mom put on her boots and coat. She reached for the door knob, but then she turned around and asked Anna something that was completely new and strange to her.

"You need some money? Wanna go out somewhere while I'm gone?"

Anna was too shocked to answer, but her mom was already reaching into her pocket. A second later, she put a fifty dollar bill on the counter, smiled, and closed the front door behind her.

What is going on? Fifty bucks? Where did mom get so much money?

But it wasn't even about the money. It was about everything. Her mom had looked normal this morning. She had acted normally…like every mom should act. She had cooked Anna breakfast!

And Anna's mom had talked to Anna normally and even called her honey! Anna felt like it was too much to process all at once. She needed to talk to someone.

She went to her room and looked for her phone. After she found it, she quickly typed a text message to Kevin asking him to meet her at the coffee shop. Anna didn't want to be alone. She wanted to be with Kevin. She wanted to talk to him. She wanted to tell him all about her Christmas morning.

Does everything that happened this morning mean mom will be better now? Is it her new job that is making her so happy?

Anna really hoped so, and she couldn't wait until the evening. She wanted to see her mom again and talk to her the next time. Yes, Anna planned to talk to her mom and ask her every single question that she currently had bouncing around her brain.

Eight

That day was very happy for Anna. She felt excited. She felt lifted up. She was in a good mood all day. She met Kevin in the coffee shop, and they talked the morning away until it was lunch time...until they both got so hungry that they each finally headed to their respective homes to eat.

Once home, Anna fixed a quick lunch for herself and even found a book to read. She rarely read, but today she just felt like doing so. The book was very interesting; it kept her occupied for a few hours until the lines and letters began to blur. Anna wasn't used to reading so much at a time. But today she made a mental note to herself that it would be good to finish this book and to get a new one from the school library. She knew that reading was good for people, and she wanted to do more good things in her life.

After reading, Anna finally did all the laundry, something that had desperately needed to be done like a month ago. Now, that she had so much cash on hand, Anna washed all of her own clothing and sheets, and she even washed most of her mom's clothing.

Between Anna's trips to the laundromat, she cleaned the entire apartment. Again, that wasn't an ordinary activity for her to do. No, she wasn't a messy person, not at all. She typically tried to clean her room once in a while, and she tried to keep her things organized, but today she also cleaned the living room, the kitchen, and even the bathroom. All the productivity made Anna feel even better. She felt so satisfied. It was just a clean apartment, but she felt like she had actually accomplished something big today.

When it had been already dark outside for a few hours, Anna started checking the clock more often. It was six o'clock, then seven, and then almost eight, but her mom wasn't home yet. Anna wished she had asked her mom what time she should expect her home, but then again, that wasn't a usual question to ask in their household. No one was expecting the other person at home. The two of them just came and went independently, like they just shared the apartment space but lived totally separate lives.

After eight o'clock, Anna felt worry start creeping in, and she hated herself for that dark emotion.

Mama said she's coming home, so I have to trust her. She meant it.

But Anna was getting anxious from all the waiting, so she decided to read more in her book. She read for about thirty minutes. For some reason, though, the book didn't seem as interesting as it had been just a few hours ago. Anna kept turning pages, but her mind was elsewhere.

Finally, Anna closed the book and went to the kitchen to look for food. She found a package of dry waffle mix and decided to make some.

Who cares that it's dinner time? I love waffles any time of the day.

Anna checked the instructions carefully and made sure to make enough mix for herself and for her mom. Then she made the waffles for herself while putting the rest of the mix in the fridge, hoping to make waffles for her mom shortly.

Anna kept thinking that her mom would show up any minute, but the minutes kept passing by, and her mom wasn't home yet. By eleven o'clock Anna felt exhausted both physically and emotionally, so she decided to lay down on the couch to wait. Anna dimmed the lights, and she didn't notice when she fell asleep.

She woke up from the noise. It was so bright in the room all of a sudden that she couldn't keep her eyes open. She covered her eyes with her hand while squinting and trying to figure out what was going on.

"What are you doing on my couch? Go to your room now!"

Anna heard her mom's voice. And then she heard someone laughing. It was a male. Both voices were loud, and the room smelled like alcohol.

Anna wanted to cry. She felt so insignificant. She felt like she just couldn't deal with this anymore. She had really hoped that her mom was getting all better and that she still loved her daughter and cared about her.

The day had started with such hope. Anna had just wanted to spend the evening with her mom, as her mom had promised. She had wanted to make waffles for her mom, and she had wanted to tell her about the new book she was reading.

Anna felt her eyes burning with tears, but she didn't want *them* to see her crying, so she quickly got up and went to her room. She shut the door tightly and fell down on her bed. The sheets smelled so clean and fresh, but Anna didn't care. She just wanted her mom to be normal again…

The noises in the living room were loud. Both her mom and the newest visitor were laughing and talking and who knows what else they were doing in there. However, Anna had learned to block these things out a long time ago.

She covered her head with the pillow, closed her eyes tightly, and tried to go back to sleep. Sleep didn't come for a long time, though, not until it became quiet in the apartment again. Then Anna finally fell asleep.

That night, Anna dreamed about her mom being loving and caring again, just like she had been for a short while in the morning.

Nine

When Anna woke up the next morning, both her mom and the new male friend were gone. The living room and the kitchen looked messy again. That was normal, though.

Why did I even bother cleaning yesterday?

Despite the gloom of her thoughts about the untidy apartment, Anna felt hungry. So, she decided to eat some breakfast. Surprisingly, most the food that her mom had bought the day before was gone.

What did they do with all the food? Did they just eat all night long?

Anna felt like crying again. She felt so much pity for herself that it was hard to handle the emotions.

What kind of mom does this? How could she? Does she not care about me at all? But I am her child! Could that not mean anything to her at all?

Anna made herself a cup of hot coffee and opened the fridge looking for the hazelnut creamer, but it was gone as well. Anna couldn't believe her eyes, so she even looked into the garbage can and saw the empty bottle in there. It was the last straw.

She burst into tears.

What did they do with the creamer? How can you finish a whole bottle in one night? Were they so drunk that they thought it was milk?

Tears were running down Anna's cheeks. She was so upset that she couldn't stop the flood any longer. It wasn't about the creamer; it was about way more than that.

The overflow of turmoil in Anna's spirit was about her mom and her inconsistent attitude and actions. It was about her mom and her lack of love and responsibility toward her own daughter. It was about her mom and her never really changing her behavior. Well, her mom's behavior was changing, but always in more negative ways.

It was just getting worse and worse with every year of Anna's life. And when Anna finally saw a slight hope to have a normal family and normal relationship with her mom as she had the day before—when her mom was home, cooked breakfast for her, and even gave her money— her mom ruined this hope once again…

That's all my mom is good for. Ruining every hope and every dream I have! I'm so done with her. I don't wanna live like this any more. I don't wanna live at all if that's what my life is going to be like.

Anna threw herself on her bed and started crying so hard that her entire body was shaking. She cried her eyes out. She cried her soul out. When she finally calmed down, she felt empty inside. Just…empty.

Anna slowly got up and realized that she had a pounding headache. Her head hurt so bad that it was hard to think.

I need some Tylenol. I hope they didn't eat the entire bottle of Tylenol last night. Who knows what else they were doing in there.

Anna went back to the kitchen on leaden feet. Her cup of coffee was still sitting on the table. She took a sip, but it was cold now. Anna reached for the top cabinet, and after moving a few things out of the way, she finally found the Tylenol bottle. She opened it and took one pill out.

Should I take two? This headache is just terrible.

Anna took another pill out and put both in her mouth and swallowed them with a few sips of the cold coffee. As she was closing the bottle, she suddenly stopped for a second and stared down at the lid of the Tylenol bottle. She stood like that for about a minute, and then she slowly opened the bottle again and shakily poured most of the bottle into her right hand. A few spilled on the floor.

Anna hastily put one more in her mouth and swallowed. Then she put one more and swallowed it even more quickly this time.

Anna wasn't thinking clearly. She felt like she was dreaming. The headache was so bad, and she just wanted it gone.

She was swallowing what she thought was her sixth or seventh pill when she felt her old Nokia vibrating in her pocket.

That brought Anna back to reality. She sat the bottle down, poured what was still in her hand back into the bottle, reached for her phone, and flipped it open.

Hi, Anny. How r u? miss you a lot! Lets meet @ the coffee shop? Love you.

Those words were enough for Anna to stop and realize what she had been doing. She shook her head and felt so embarrassed.

What have I done? Oh my goodness! What have I done? How many pills did I take?!

Anna couldn't remember exactly how many she had taken, but she felt so scared. Her heart seemed to be pounding as hard as her head.

I don't want to die. No! I want to live!

There was so much more to Anna's life than her miserable mom! Anna had Kevin, and they had been in love since they were kids. They had something rare and amazing—she knew it, and in a moment, she had almost ruined her life by being so stupid.

Anna texted Kevin back.

C u in 30 min. I miss you too. Love u > anything.

Anna went to her bedroom to get dressed. She kept thinking about the pills that she had swallowed. She hoped that she hadn't taken enough to cause damage. The bottle still looked almost full, so it had to be okay. It just had to be.

When Anna left her apartment ten minutes later, she was feeling better. Her headache was going away.

Ten

Anna walked to the coffee shop very quickly. It was bitingly cold outside, and she desperately wanted to see Kevin. She knew that she would be there faster than Kevin by walking so fast, which meant she would have to wait for him. She hated waiting. But today she didn't have a choice.

Short of breath and with burning cheeks, red nose, and cold hands, Anna opened the front door of the coffee shop.

Anna walked inside and gasped. There they were again—her mom and another version of her, Anna—they were literally standing right in front of her. Anna couldn't believe her eyes.

This time, the teenage girl was wearing tight jeans and a red sweater. She was holding her coat in her left hand and her drink in her right. Her mom was wearing a nice winter dress and high heels. Her hair was down, and she had a heavy necklace on. Everything about these two looked fancy and expensive. They both looked like they just left a hairdresser and a very expensive boutique.

"Ann, darling, you have to be nicer to him. He is your dad after all!" her mom was saying.

"Oh, whatever! I don't care. I'm still too upset to even talk to him." Anna heard the girl answer.

"But that was like a month ago, honey. You have to let it go. Please talk to him. He called me again last night. He really wants to see you."

"I don't think so."

"Ann, do this for me, please."

Anna was standing at the doorway staring at the two as they were talking and leaving the coffee shop. They didn't even glance at her, like Anna wasn't even there.

The other girl reached for the front door and brushed Anna with her shoulder without apparently noticing.

Anna stood there for another split second, but this time she decided to follow them right away. She got the door as her mom was still holding it, and she immediately followed them outside.

It wasn't so cold now. Anna was surprised as she had been freezing cold on her way to the coffee shop, but now it was even a little sunny and warm. No wonder the other girl didn't wear her coat but was still holding it in her hand.

Anna watched her mom and the girl get into a car. It was a brand-new-looking silver Mercedes. The other girl rolled her window down as she was still saying something to her mom.

"Just stop bugging me about it already. I told you I'm not talking to him. He can come and apologize if he wants to talk to me that much!"

"But he did apologize, Ann, don't you re…" That was all Anna could hear as the Mercedes pulled out of the parking lot.

Anna stood there feeling shocked and disoriented again. She couldn't make sense of what she had seen. She saw a girl who looked just like her, and she saw a nicer version of her mom but how much sense did that make?

Anna slowly turned around and saw Kevin. Finally he was here. But what was that new haircut about?

"Hey, Kevin. What did you do to your hair?"

"Hi, Ann. Um…I didn't do anything. How are you?" Kevin's voice sounded strange, but Anna couldn't pinpoint why it sounded strange.

"What do you mean you didn't do anything to your hair? You cut it! When did you cut it and why so short?!"

"Ann, my hair has always been like that. But it's strange that you even noticed my hair."

"What? What do you mean it's strange I even noticed your hair? Are you kidding me? I love your hair, and I love touching it!"

"You do?" Kevin looked surprised.

"What is wrong with you today? Why do you look so shocked? Like you're surprised to see me or something?"

"No, I'm not surprised to see you. That's why I came here. I am surprised you're talking to me, though."

"Why wouldn't I talk to you?"

"I don't know. Why wouldn't you? Is it because I'm sick?"

"What? Are you sick? You didn't tell me you were sick!" Anna felt mad at him. He was acting so strange.

"Ann, I told you."

"When? Let's go inside and talk like adults. You're driving me crazy today, Kevin."

Kevin opened the door and let her in first. Anna stepped inside and turned around, but Kevin was gone.

Anna froze. She was too confused to understand where he had gone because he clearly had been holding the door for her just a second ago. Then she heard his voice again and saw him sitting at their usual table.

"Anny! Finally! What took you so long?"

Anna looked at Kevin. He was coming toward her. He had his normal long hair, which was partially covering his eyes as usual.

How could this be?

"Kevin, um…hi. Your hair?"

"What about it?"

"Nothing, it's nothing. Are you sick, Kevin?"

"Me? No, I'm not sick. But you don't look too well. Are you okay? Where have you been? I texted you and called you. But nothing. I've been waiting for almost two hours now!"

"Two hours?" Anna was shocked.

"Yes! Are you okay?"

"Yes, yes, I'm fine. I'm very thirsty though. Let me go get some iced water and then we can sit down and talk."

Anna went to order iced water. It was Robin working today, and Anna was very glad to see her.

Then she went to the bathroom and looked in the mirror.

What in the world is going on? My mom and that girl whose name is Ann and who looks just like me..how can that be?

And now Kevin? What's that all about? How can Kevin have been waiting for me for almost two hours in here when I was only gone from the shop for less than five minutes? But he is right, it's almost one o'clock now!

Oh, my goodness! What is going on?

Anna stood there for a minute more, looking into the mirror and thinking. Then she washed her face with cold water and went back out to talk to Kevin.

She decided to ignore all of it. Absolutely everything. She would pretend like it had never happened. And hopefully it would never happen again.

But little did she know…

Eleven

One week had gone by, and everything seemed to be back to normal—normal in Anna's sense. Winter break was over, and school was starting back again. Anna was looking forward to her Chemistry class and not so much to all her other classes. She had finished the book she started reading over the winter break, but she never went to the library to get herself a new one.

Anna's mom came home every night, but she was always drunk, and she had that same new friend with her a couple of times. They were loud at night, but at least both of them were gone in the morning.

Anna spent a lot of time with Kevin. They saw each other every day; he came to visit her a few times, and she went to see him and his family as well. Kevin's little sister Lauren loved Anna and got excited every time she was visiting.

One day even Kevin's mom was at home. Elizabeth worked so much that Anna rarely saw her. However, that day Elizabeth was off and had cooked a special family dinner. She was so kind to Anna and insisted on her staying for dinner.

Anna stayed even though she felt a little uncomfortable. Afterward, she was happy that she had stayed as they all had very nice time together. Kevin's family was so different from her own.

It was only the oldest sister Katie who didn't belong there, but this idea was only Anna's opinion. It seemed that Elizabeth, Kevin, and Lauren all loved Katie as much as they all loved each other.

Anna really wanted to go to the coffee shop. It had been her almost daily routine for many years now, but she was too nervous about what might happen or what she might see. She didn't go for five days because she was afraid that strange things would happen again.

But then Anna finally felt calm enough to go again. She decided to visit the coffee shop the day before school started again. It was a nice, sunny winter day outside. Anna enjoyed her slow walk and even unbuttoned her coat as she was getting too warm with it buttoned. The rare temperate weather definitely didn't feel like January.

When Anna approached the coffee shop, she quickly noticed a silver Mercedes in the parking lot, and she got very nervous again for a moment. She just stood there looking at the car, but shortly, she saw a man in a black suit walking toward the Mercedes. He was clean-cut looking and a very young woman was following him. They both got into the car and took off. Anna felt relieved.

Inside the coffee shop, Anna felt good. She liked this place more than she liked her home. She still had some money left from that one morning when her mom had been sober and cooked breakfast for her. So, Anna decided to treat herself, ordered a cappuccino, and went to take her usual seat in the dark corner.

It was busy at the shop. Almost every table was taken, and there were a few people waiting for their drinks. Anna loved observing people—their interactions with each other, the way that they were dressed, the drinks that they ordered.

Anna sipped slowly on her cappuccino, and when she was done with it, she took out her old notebook and pencils from her backpack. She started drawing. Anna wasn't very good at it if anyone asked her; it was "just a hobby."

Anna had heard from others, especially from Kevin, that her drawings were great and that she should take a drawing class in school. Anna promised Kevin a few times that she would take a class, but she never did. She couldn't even explain to herself why she hadn't. Maybe it was because drawing was hers alone. It wasn't something for others to see, although they sometimes did see her art, but she didn't do it to be graded or critiqued. Anna simply drew because she enjoyed creating art, and it was all hers.

Today, Anna didn't have any idea what she wanted to draw. She took a pencil and started with simple lines. She kept drawing and soon enough, she had a image in her head that she was trying to put down on the paper. She kept drawing and erasing, then drawing more, and about an hour later, it was completed. Anna was looking at Kevin's face in her notebook. She was satisfied. The drawing was really good, and Anna smiled as she looked down at it.

Anna had drawn Kevin many times before, and he had even convinced her to give him several of her works to keep. However, this one was different. In it, Kevin's hair was short and his face was thinner. Kevin's face looked just as Anna had seen it that day outside of the coffee shop when he told her that he was surprised that she was talking to him and that he was sick.

Twelve

*A*nna saw them again. She was at the coffee shop spending time after school, and when she came back from the bathroom, there they were—sitting at the same table as they had been before. It seemed like they always were seated at that particular table. It was located across the coffee shop, so there was enough distance in between them, allowing Anna to observe and even hear some conversation parts.

This time they were arguing. Her mom was obviously upset with the other teenage girl, Ann didn't seem to care much. Anna heard phrases such as "but he is your dad!" and "you can't ignore him forever" as well as "I don't care" and "I'm too mad at him."

They left shortly, and Anna didn't attempt to follow them this time. She was simply too nervous. She stayed in the coffee shop while thinking about it all.

Why is that Ann so mad at her dad? Is Ann me but in a different life? How is it possible? It seems like they're living a rich life…But still they don't look too happy…

Ann has a dad. I have a dad in that life! But she's too mad at him for whatever reason. I wish I had a dad in this life…I would never be mad enough at him to not talk to him. But, then again, who knows what kind of dad he is and what has he done?

Kevin is there as well but Ann doesn't talk to him either. I don't talk to him in that life! Wow, it's just too strange to think about her as me. I wonder what's wrong with that Kevin. He told me he's sick, and he looked so sad. And so skinny…

Anna kept contemplating everything she had found out so far. She wondered if other people at the coffee shop had seen Anny and her mom. She pondered about it for a while and then decided to ask Robin.

"Excuse me, Robin. Do you have a second?"

"Hey, you. I always have a second for you. What can I do for you, sweetie?"

"Robin, have you seen two people from that table? They left like thirty minutes ago? It was a lady wearing black pants and purple shirt and a teenage girl in jeans and bright pink sweater. I found something that I think they lost, and I was just wondering if you know them. Seems like they come here often."

"Um…I'm not sure I know who you're talking about. It has been so busy today and this week overall, but I don't recall seeing the two you described. What did they forget? I can keep it here in case they come back for it."

"Oh no, that's okay. It's really nothing. I'll just give it back to them the next time I see them. You know I'm here like every day anyway. Thanks for the help, Robin."

"I didn't help much, but okay."

Anna went back to her table. Now she was wondering if Robin didn't see those two or if she had just forgotten. It was a very busy coffee shop, like Robin said. But still…it was strange.

Anna was planning to meet Kevin in the coffee shop that evening, and this time she finally felt brave enough to tell him about the mysterious events that has been happening to her.

At first, Kevin listened seriously, but then as Anna continued with her story, he burst out laughing.

"Anny, I love your sense of humor, and I love all your creativity, but that's just insane. Your story's not even close to being realistic enough for me to believe it."

Anna's cheeks flushed, and she got very defensive.

"I'm not lying! I'm telling you the truth! I saw them, Kevin, I promise. I saw myself, and I saw my mom as well as I saw you! But, like I said, you looked different. You were sad and skinny. You had short hair and you told me that I didn't talk to you. I mean, that the other Anna…I mean, she was called Ann…didn't talk to you."

"Anna, just listen to yourself. It makes no sense!"

"I know it doesn't! That's why I'm trying to figure it all out! Isn't it strange that you had to wait for me for a while both times when I went to that side, but I felt like I only spent seconds and minutes on that side!?!"

"So, now there is *that* side? That's what you're going to call it? *That* side, *that* Ann, *that* Kevin…?"

"Listen to me! I need your help. I know I saw everything I told you about. Please help me understand. Please help me understand if that's all real or if I'm losing my mind. I need to know if anybody else can see them when they come here."

"Okay, okay. You know I would do anything for you. But what exactly you want me to do?"

"Just keep coming here with me, and I will tell you when I see them again."

"Is that all?"

"Yes. Well…I really wanna go to that side again."

"Why?"

"To see you, Kevin! I can't tell you enough how very sad you looked there. My heart breaks thinking about you that way. I really need to see you on that side again and talk to you more."

"Anna, just listen to what you're saying…I'm right here with you!"

"Kevin! You said you would do this for me."

"Oh, dear…Okay. I will."

Anna looked Kevin straight in the eyes, and she knew in that moment that he meant it. He would do anything for her. And Anna would do anything for Kevin. She loved him with all her heart, and she always would.

But Anna's tender heart was aching for that other Kevin as well who was sick and maybe even completely alone…She needed to see him again. She just had to.

Thirteen

Days went by, and nothing happened. Anna went to the coffee shop almost every day, and she dragged Kevin with her. They spent hours at a time at the coffee shop—waiting and waiting some more. But nobody showed up. That other Ann and her mom were not coming to the coffee shop anymore. Anna was hoping to see Kevin, that other Kevin, but she had only seen him that once, the previous time when she had been on the other side.

It was the end of the February, and Anna had almost convinced herself that none of it had been real. It had never happened. She never saw the people. It had all been her imagination.

Kevin was working hard on convincing her as well. He kept coming to the coffee shop with her as he had promised her, but he kept telling her that she was just very stressed with her mom being good for one day and then disappearing again, and that's why she imagined "the alternative life" where her mom was normal and they were rich and happy.

Anna was very close to believing Kevin's theory, but all it took was looking at the drawing of that other Kevin she had created, and she knew immediately that it could not simply be her imagination. That other side was real, and she had seen them.

By March, Kevin started leaving the coffee shop early. He would still come with her every single time as he had promised. However, then he would leave shortly, and he encouraged Anna to go home as well. But Anna didn't want to go home. Nothing had changed at home, and if it had, it had become even worse.

Anna's mom had a new friend again, and she came home with him almost every single night. That meant that Anna was sleep deprived because they were always loud at night, and Anna hated taking naps during the day. So, she simply avoided her home. She went to school; she went to visit Kevin, and they would go for walks. But it was still too chilly and too rainy outside for long walks, and, of course, she went to the coffee shop.

Kevin started looking for a job. He was anxiously waiting for his birthday in April and was dreaming about working after school. That became his excuse for leaving her at the coffee shop. Kevin went looking for jobs almost every day, and he filled out numerous applications, but nobody seemed to want to start the hiring process before his sixteenth birthday.

Anna advised Kevin to be patient and to wait instead of wasting time and feeling frustrated. Kevin didn't want to wait, however. He wanted to find a job. He wanted to make money. He wanted to help his family, and he wanted to buy a car.

Anna was proud of Kevin. He was such a good person. He was good at everything. He was good at school. He was a good son and brother, and he was an amazing friend and boyfriend for her.

But Anna felt sad and jealous as well. She knew that finding a job would mean less time together for them. Of course, Anna and Kevin would see each other at school and on his days off, but they would not be able to spend as much time together as they had been doing.

Also, Kevin would be sixteen five months earlier than Anna would be and that just wasn't fair because Anna wanted to have a job as well. Anna was so tired of scrounging for money all over her apartment and hoping that her mom was drunk enough to have left behind some cash. Yes, that's exactly what Anna was hoping for because it was her only way of getting any money. She was so tired of not knowing what to do with herself every day after school and on the weekends. She wanted to have a job so that she would have a place to go and be productive there. But she needed to wait while Kevin was almost sixteen already…

One evening, while Anna was sitting at the coffee shop and thinking about all these facts, she heard someone opening the front door, and then she felt cold air coming her way. That was strange because it hadn't cold outside on her way to the coffee shop.

Anna turned around and felt her heart rate speeding up. No, her heart was actually racing by now. She was looking at her mom and the other teenage girl, Ann. They looked happy, dressed very nicely as before and were holding their expensive handbags. Anna knew how much these handbags cost because she had seen them at higher end stores, such as Macy's and Nordstrom, and she couldn't imagine how some people could afford accessories like that.

"Let's just get the drinks and go, okay darling?" Anna heard her mom saying.

"You don't wanna stay here for a bit?" Ann responded.

"No, I have lots to do at home."

"You will be working late from home again?"

"Yes, I'm afraid so."

The other girl looked deflated for a second, but then she smiled at her mom with her beautiful white teeth. Anna saw them both ordering lattes with almond milk and then going back to the front door.

Anna stood up immediately, grabbed her backpack, and followed the two outside. She was quick enough to grab the front door while her mom was still touching it. And just like that Anna was on the other side again. She knew it immediately because it was very cold outside. Anna wished she had her coat with her, but it had been too warm for a coat on her side of reality.

Anna stood there watching her mom and Ann getting into their fancy car and taking off.

Going to their fancy home probably... To their fancy life...

Anna didn't know what to do once they were out of sight, so she started walking slowly down the street, looking at the buildings, looking at people. She felt very strange because everything looked the same, yet it all still looked slightly different. She felt like she was in her hometown, yet she wasn't so sure...So, she kept walking and kept looking, kept hoping to see a familiar face.

And then Anna did. She saw that one familiar face. She was so shocked and so happy at the same time that she didn't know what to do with herself. She saw Kevin! He was slowly walking toward her, but he was on the other side of the street. Anna hesitated for just a second, and then she went straight to him.

After Kevin's initial surprise at seeing Anna and their greetings, she told him everything that was happening, and he listened. Kevin listened with his heart, and Anna knew that this Kevin believed her. He believed every single word that Anna told him. He didn't think she was crazy. He thought that it all was very cool actually.

And then this Kevin told Anna his story. His story was sad, too sad for Anna to hear and handle without tears, so she listened and cried while he kept talking. He had dated the Ann from his reality. They had known each other since they there kids, just like Anna knew her Kevin.

This Kevin had thought that this reality's Ann really loved him like she had always told him, but as Ann's family was getting richer and richer, Kevin's family was still poor and life was worse every year.

This Kevin's dad had also died a few years ago, and since that time, things were not so great for this Kevin and his family. His mom worked hard, but the money she brought in wasn't enough to support the family.

Kevin dreamed about finding a job when he turned sixteen, and he had still been dating Ann as of last year. But then something terrible happened. He became ill and his diagnosis wasn't promising: he had leukemia.

And that is when Ann had broken up with him. She didn't really explain why to him, but Kevin was convinced that it was because of him being so poor and so sick. Kevin still loved Ann and tried talking to her from time to time. However, she became more and more distant to him.

Now Kevin was almost sixteen, and he still dreamed of finding a job, but he wasn't sure anymore if he would be strong enough to work. The leukemia was making him sicker and weaker every week.

As they were walking, Kevin was still talking, and Anna was still crying. She didn't know that a person could cry for so long. She thought that one should run out of tears by now, but tears kept coming on their own, and she wasn't able to stop them.

"Oh, Kevin…" She didn't know what to say. It was too hard. It was too complicated, and it was too strange. His reality was so sad for him while her reality was so sad for her. She wanted to help him, but she didn't know how…

"It's okay, Anna, don't cry. I actually feel so much better now after I talked to you. I really hope I will see you again. Will you come again?"

"Of course I will!" she replied without even thinking.

"How does it work? How do you come to this side?"

"I'm not sure, to be honest. But it seems that I can come here if Ann and her mom are at the coffee shop, and then I got back home when you were with me that last time."

"I think you should go back. You look so cold. I'm afraid you will get sick after today."

"Yeah, it was definitely warmer at home when I was leaving my house."

"How will I know when I can see you again, Anna?"

"I don't know. I haven't had enough time to figure all this out, but I will be coming to the coffee shop every single day. I promise. If I see them again, I will follow them right away. But how will I find you?"

"Let me write down my address for you. It's just ten minutes away from here. Do you have a pen?"

"No, I don't. Just tell me your address, and I'll memorize it."

So, Kevin told her his address, and then he described how to find the house. He gave her as many details as he could, hoping that she would be able to find it the next time she was on his side again.

Then Kevin opened the front door to the coffee shop and told Anna to go home. She stood there, not ready to go yet. She wanted to say something else. She wanted to promise that she would come back. She wanted to tell him that she loved him, but she didn't feel like she had the right words for everything that she was feeling.

So, Anna slowly leaned closer to Kevin and kissed him. She hoped that her kiss said it all. Then Anna looked at Kevin one last time and she saw in his eyes that he understood everything she wanted to tell him. She went inside the coffee shop, and just like that, Kevin was gone.

Anna stood there for a second, feeling cold, feeling hungry, and feeling lost and confused overall. Then she felt her phone vibrating, so she took it out from her pocket and saw eighteen messages from Kevin and twenty six missed calls. She read his last text message.

I hope u r ok! Im freaking out! I dont know what to think! U didn't come 2 school for 2 days, u r not answering and u r not @ home! call me asap please please please. Love you.

Anna looked at the clock. It was seven o'clock in the evening, and that seemed about right. She had only left the coffee shop around five. Then she looked at the calendar and felt her stomach fall.

Where did the last two days go?!

Anna didn't have an answer to that question, but she knew that all that had happened would be very hard to explain to her Kevin in this reality.

Fourteen

Anna texted Kevin right away, telling him that she was okay and that she was sorry. She also promised to tell him everything at school the next day.

Kevin agreed to wait, and Anna went home. She felt exhausted physically and emotionally. Her head and her feet hurt.

When Anna got home, she was happy to be alone. She took a long hot shower, and then after a light dinner, she went straight to bed, even though it wasn't even nine o'clock.

Anna felt asleep immediately, and even if her mom came home with the newest male friend, Anna was too tired to hear anything that night.

In the morning, Anna heard her alarm going off but she still felt too drained to get up. She turned it off and went back to sleep. When Anna finally woke up, it was almost ten in the morning, and her head hurt more than it had the night before. Anna's throat was burning, and she had a runny nose. She was coming down with a cold. That meant that she would miss even more school. But she didn't care.

Anna did care about Kevin, though. He was probably mad at her by this point. She grabbed her phone and checked for any text messages from him. There were a few, and it didn't seem that Kevin was mad. Instead, he was worrying about her and maybe frustrated at her for not being at school again, but he wasn't mad. Or she just hoped so.

Anna texted Kevin and said that she was really sick and couldn't come to school. Kevin responded immediately, saying that he would come to see her after school. Anna agreed to that plan and went to check for any food in the kitchen.

To Anna's surprised, there was a pack of fresh eggs in the fridge and a new bottle of milk. That made her smile. Anna was ready for a good breakfast, so she busied herself with making an omelet and coffee with fresh milk.

The food tasted delicious. It tasted so good, like she hasn't eaten anything for a couple of days. And Anna knew very well what it meant not to eat for a couple of days…

Anna's headache didn't go away even after the breakfast, so she took some Tylenol and went back to bed. Anna was laying down with her eyes closed but she wasn't sleeping. She was recalling everything that had happened the day before.

Anna remembered the moment when she first saw Kevin on the other side of the street. She remembered exactly how he had looked. He was so skinny, so weak, so sad… She looked at him in that moment, and she knew that he wasn't feeling well and that he was very lonely.

Anna went to him, and when he saw her, he looked confused. "Ann?"

"Hi, Kevin."

"You look different." Anna smiled at his observation.

"Not so fancy, ha?" she asked.

"No, no, that's not what I meant. You just look different. But you look very lovely!"

"Well…you look different yourself." Now she made Kevin smile.

"Do I look worse? Sicker?" he asked.

"Kevin, that's not what I meant either. Do you know who I am?"

"I hope I do! You're Ann. I've known you most of my life! We used to love each other, and we used to date. Until I got sick. And poor."

"I am Anna. Or Anny. But I prefer Anna. But I'm not your Ann. I'm like a different version of her. I live in a different reality." Kevin was staring at her by this point.

"What do you mean, a different reality? What are you talking about?"

"Do you remember seeing me like this before? When I looked different like I do now?"

"Um…yes, that was a like a month or two ago. By the coffee shop, your favorite one." Kevin was still staring intently at her, like he was studying a foreign object, like he was trying to understand what was going on.

"Yes, that was me. But I'm not your Ann. Not the one you used to love and date."

"Oh, wait a second. I still love her! She's the one…I mean, you're the one who stopped loving me. Only it's not you? I'm confused now. Can you start from the very beginning?"

So, Anna started from the very beginning. Anna told him about the magical White Christmas and how she had seen the other Ann and her mom at the coffee shop for the first time. Kevin listened to every word Anna told him, and she saw in his eyes that he trusted her. He didn't question her. He didn't tell her that she was being insane or even illogical. He just trusted her, as simple as that. Anna immediately felt a deep, abiding sympathy for this Kevin.

Anna started to wonder if she actually loved this Kevin. And if someone asked her, she didn't feel guilty about it. Anna knew that she was in love with her reality's Kevin, and this boy was the very same Kevin. He was just on the other side, in a different reality. The other side had become a common phrase for Anna by now, and she referred to it frequently in her own mind and aloud to her own Kevin. As illogical and as crazy as this all sounded, she couldn't help it.

Now Anna was resting in the bed, thinking about the previous day, about her conversation with that other reality's Kevin, trying to ponder every detail and every word he had told her.

Anna remembered his story. How could she not? It was sad and heartbreaking. His dad dying and his mom working hard and struggling to provide for the family had made her cry for him.

That Kevin's devastating diagnosis and his mom trying her best to take him to all his appointments and her troubles with all his medical bills had made Anna cry further.

Kevin feeling guilty because he felt he had become such a burden to his family, even though nobody ever told him that made Anna cry even more.

Then, when that Kevin had told her about his reality's Anny breaking up with him and the pain being worse than even his leukemia diagnosis, Anna had felt her heart truly breaking.

Laying in the bed and recalling that deep conversation, Anna was in tears again. Her tender heart and thoughts were upon that Kevin's struggles and pain, wanting nothing more than to comfort him and to make him happy.

Anna didn't know when she was going to see that Kevin again, though, and she didn't know how to help him, but she felt determined to do everything possible to help. Anna knew that it was the right thing to do, and she wanted to do the right thing, at least this one time in her life.

It was almost two in the afternoon. Anna knew that her Kevin would be coming soon to see her after school. She would be happy to see him, but she was anxious at the same time. She didn't know how much she should or could tell him. She wanted to tell him everything. She really did…but she wasn't sure he would believe her story.

Anna was nervous that her Kevin would try to convince her once again that it was all in her imagination—probably because she was sick right now. *What a perfect excuse!* Anna waited anxiously for Kevin to show up while still trying to decide how much to tell him.

Fifteen

"Anna, not again…please." Kevin's face looked pained.
"What do you mean by not again?!" Anna exclaimed, becoming agitated.

"Your stories about the other side don't sound very convincing."

"Do you think I'm crazy, Kevin? Just tell me—is that what you really think?!" Anna was almost yelling by her last question. She wanted Kevin to believe her, and she felt helpless because she didn't know how to convince him or if she could.

"I'm not saying that you're crazy. I'm just saying, everything you're telling me sounds a little crazy and very illogical. Plus, I never was able to see that other side and all those people from the other side."

"Really? So, that's your reason? It's simply because *you* didn't see them? And you know why you didn't, Kevin? You wanna know why?!"

Kevin looked tired, tired from arguing with her. And that made Anna even madder. She felt like she was on fire. That's how mad she was.

"No. Why? I guess you know why, and you really wanna tell me." His voice was steady and calm.

"Yes, you're right, I wanna tell you! It's because you promised me to go to the coffee shop with me, but then you stopped coming or you came and left right away. You didn't keep your promise." Tears welled up in Anna's eyes. Oh, how mad she was at him for not having kept his promise!

"Anna, I came as long as I could, and I stayed as long as I could, but there are other things in life that I wanna do. You know I'm looking for a job. You know how important it is for me."

"Any luck?!" Anna felt like she was being cruel to him.

"No. You know they all want me to be sixteen."

"Oh really? And you just found that out? Didn't I tell you to stop wasting your time and efforts? Just wait another month, and then apply."

Anna was looking at Kevin like she was daring him. She felt disgusted inside. She didn't have to be that cruel to him. She loved him after all! But that boy knew how to make her mad!

She kept looking at Kevin, waiting for him to say something, but he remained quiet. He looked so sad that suddenly she wanted to take all her harsh words back.

Anna wanted to hug and kiss him. She wanted to tell him how much she loved him. She wanted to tell him that his opinion mattered to her and that's why it was so important for her to have his trust and understanding. She wanted to tell him more about the other Kevin. She wanted to tell him how much she wanted to help him…but she didn't say any of it.

Anna wanted Kevin to say something first. She was waiting.

But Kevin didn't say anything. He slowly got up from the couch and went to the front door.

"Are you leaving?" Anna heard her hoarse voice. It sounded like it wasn't even her own—like someone else was talking.

"I think it's better if I leave, Anna."

"Okay, whatever you want!"

"That's not what I want. I want to be with you, but you act like you don't wanna be with me. You disappear for two days, and then you tell me some crazy things expecting me to believe you. That's enough, Anna. I'm sorry."

"That's enough? Enough of what? Of our relationship? Is that what you mean?" Anna felt like she was losing control and would start crying any second. But she was still too mad and frustrated with him. She didn't want him to see her cry. She didn't know anymore what she wanted.

"Call me when you feel ready to talk." Kevin's tone was quiet.

Doesn't he care?! How can he be so calm? Doesn't he understand?

And in the next moment, Kevin was gone.

Anna couldn't control herself for another second. She burst into tears. She knew that crying wouldn't help, but she didn't know what would.

Sixteen

The next several weeks flew by, and Kevin turned sixteen. Anna celebrated his birthday with him by going to the coffee shop and ordering their favorite drinks and nice desserts. She had been saving up for his day by setting aside coins and dollar bills since Christmas. Kevin was really against Anna paying for them, but she was able to convince him that it was her birthday present for him, so he finally gave in, and they both enjoyed the evening at the coffee shop.

Anna was quiet and nervous, and felt very tense for the first hour or so. She was nervous that strange things would happen again and she just didn't want them to happen today. The day when Anna had argued with Kevin about going to the other side was still fresh in her memory, and she didn't want that to happen again, especially on his special day.

After that argument, Anna had decided to keep the other side completely to herself. After thinking about everything that had been happening, she finally accepted that she shouldn't tell anyone because people would not understand. Even Kevin didn't understand and didn't believe her. It was a hard decision to make, but she did make it. The other side was a little secret from now on, and it was only hers to keep.

Anna kept coming to the coffee shop, but she stopped inviting Kevin, other than for his birthday. They went other places together. It was getting warmer outside each day, so they enjoyed walks in the park and on the streets. They went to the coffee shop together just a few times, but it was always very quick.

Anna was afraid to see her mom and Ann there. She knew that she would follow them again in order to go see that other Kevin, and she knew that it would mean another argument with her Kevin. But on the days that Anna wasn't meeting with Kevin or when he was busy looking for a job, she went to the coffee shop on her own, and she spent hours there waiting. She would be the last customer to leave, and she didn't even care about ordering only an iced water. She couldn't help it; she just wanted to see them again.

But nothing happened since that last time. Anna didn't see her mom or Ann again. She didn't know why. She didn't understand how this thing worked, and she felt helpless. But today, today was different. Today was Kevin's birthday, and she didn't want any surprises.

"Thanks for this present. I feel special." Kevin smiled one of his handsome smiles.

"It's nothing. I wish I could buy you something, a real gift. But this should be the last year. Next year it will be different. It will be better, much better. We're both going to work and make money. Can you just imagine that? Getting paid every other week! Or every week! Wow…that sounds amazing. And unrealistic if you ask me." Anna burst out laughing.

"Yeah, that'll be so cool."

"By the way, I love this latte with organic almond milk. I feel so fancy drinking this. When I do work, I'll buy myself one of these every single day."

"Then you will get fat." Kevin laughed.

"What? No, I won't!" Anna knew that he was just being silly.

"Guess what?" now he was smiling like he knew something that she didn't.

"What?"

"Take a guess." Kevin's smile was getting broader with each passing second.

"What? I don't know! Just tell me! Kevin, you have to tell me! What is it?" Anna demanded for him to tell her, but he clearly enjoyed every moment of it, being in control.

"Oh c'mon, any ideas?"

"You're terrible, I hope you know that!" Anna was staring at Kevin.

"So you're giving up without even trying?"

"Wait a second. No way…You got a job?!" Anna's eyes got bigger as she looked at Kevin while trying to understand if her guess was correct.

"Yes!" Kevin looked so grown up all of a sudden. Anna couldn't believe it was her Kevin sitting in front of her. Didn't they go to Kindergarten together? Wasn't he the same boy that used to come to school with the same avocado sandwich every single day and everyone was making fun of him? Everyone but her. She just understood that he loved avocados! Wasn't he the first boy who kissed her? Well…he was the only boy who had ever kissed her. And now he was sitting in front of her telling her that he got a job!

"Kevin, oh my goodness! Where at? I can't believe you didn't tell me!"

"It just happened today. I had an interview right after school."

"And they hired you right away?" Anna was surprised.

"I know, right? Well, they have to do a background check and some paperwork, but if everything comes back normal...and I know it will, then the job is mine!"

"Congratulations! That's awesome! My boyfriend has a job now. That's probably the best birthday gift ever!" Anna was truly happy for him. Also, she knew that she would be next to get a job. She just needed to be patient and wait another few months.

"Don't you wanna know where your boyfriend works now?"

"Of course, I wanna know! I'm just too excited!"

"It's at Slice of Italy Pizza. I can work there after school and on the weekends."

"Are you serious? That's the best pizza place around here! Wow, I'm so impressed! How did you get a job there?"

"I wanna say that it's all because I'm so cool and simply amazing, but it's actually because of my dad. The owner used to work with my dad a long time ago. He recognized the last name on my application and decided to call. When I went there, we talked about my family and my dad more than anything else. I think it'll be a very nice place to work at. Also, he said that eventually I can deliver pizza. I just need to get a driver's license and to make enough money to buy a car."

Anna was listening to him talking, but she felt like it couldn't real. It sounded too good, like a fairy tale. Maybe not to other people, to normal people. But to her, with her broken life...everything sounded amazing. Still, Anna was truly happy for Kevin.

That evening Kevin walked her home. They strolled slowly, enjoying every second of it, holding hands until it was time to say goodbye. On the way, they talked more about Kevin's new job, and they talked about their future.

Anna and Kevin definitely saw each other being together. They had been inseparable since Kindergarten, and they didn't think anything would ever change that. They never talked about getting married or anything; they knew that they were still kids, but deep in their hearts, they just knew that they belonged together, and nothing would ever change that.

Seventeen

The months of April and May flew by for Kevin, but for Anna, it felt like the two months lasted forever. Kevin started working at the Slice of Italy Pizzeria, and the job occupied the majority of his free time. Anna still saw Kevin at school every day, and they always ate lunch together, but she desperately missed their after school time together. She missed their walks in the park and on the streets; she missed their visits to the coffee shop, and she missed Kevin's visits at her home.

Now Anna's home was more lonely than ever before. Mom wasn't showing up every night, but at least her last new friend was a long time gone now. She had found a new one, but he only lasted for a week or so. And Anna was happy about that. She never liked her mom's friends. All they were good for was destroying food and creating a mess. Oh, and loud noises at night…

Anna knew that Kevin felt bad that he spent all his free time working, including the weekends, but Anna always told him that it was fine, and she truly meant that. She knew how much Kevin wanted to work because that's as much as she wanted to work herself.

Anna tried to occupy her after school hours with reading books. That activity was new for her. She had never been a big reader. She had read a book here and there, but lately she read one book after another, and she found a lot of pleasure in reading. And, of course, she read at the coffee shop. Anna went there every single day now, reading her books and waiting.

Days were passing by, and Anna found it hard to believe that she used to see her mom and Ann there. It was hard to believe in the other side all together, but she kept coming and waiting. In fact, Anna kept coming to the coffee shop until it finally happened again.

Anna would be able to get to the other side once again! She couldn't believe her eyes when she finally saw the two, but she watched avidly. Her mom looked slightly tired but as gorgeous as before. Ann, on the other hand, looked happy and didn't stop talking even for one second while they were waiting for their to-go drinks. She kept talking to her mom, telling her about this one boy; his name was James and apparently he was amazing at everything. To Anna, it looked like her mom was a little annoyed with the topic, but she didn't say anything and kept listening and nodding.

When they got their drinks and were ready to go, Anna stood up, ready to follow them. She kept her head low and pretended to look down at her phone. Anna wasn't sure if they were able to see her, but to be honest, she felt like even if they were, they would never notice someone like her. However, she still didn't want to attract any attention. All she wanted was to get to the other side in order to see that Kevin.

Once had Anna grabbed the door while it was still open and stepped outside, she knew immediately that the shift had worked.

She was on the other side. She just felt it. Everything was slightly off. Even the air felt different. It was hard to explain why it was different. She just knew it.

So, Anna stood for a few moments trying to adjust to this other reality, and then she started walking. She was heading directly toward Kevin's house, and she was well prepared for it. She had memorized his address, and she had already checked that same address location in her own reality.

The house was little but looked very nice from outside. Anna had gone to see that house several times in the last two months. She wasn't sure why exactly she kept going there because she definitely had learned the direction after the very first time, and it wasn't like the other Kevin lived there in her own reality. It was just another thing that she didn't have a good explanation for.

In a few short minutes, Anna was standing in front of the house, and like everything else, it looked slightly different from what she had seen in her own reality. It wasn't as good looking, but it was still recognizable.

There was a different car parked on the driveway, and the automobile was much older. Everything at the address looked like people who lived there didn't have enough time to make things look presentable. And Anna knew very well that it was true—with Kevin's dad being gone, his mom working hard, and Kevin being sick.

Then Anna was standing by the front door, but she didn't have enough courage to knock.

What will I say if Kevin's mom opens the door?

But the more Anna stood there, the more she realized that she didn't have any other choice. She finally was there and she needed to act. So, she knocked quietly and even closed her eyes in anticipation.

"Hey, you…Is that you, Anna? I can't believe I'm seeing you again." It was Kevin's voice she was hearing, and it sounded so good! She opened her eyes.

"Kevin…" Anna didn't know what else to say, but she was so happy to finally see him again. She looked at him closer, and her heart ached from what she saw. Kevin's hair was all gone and he looked so skinny and so weak. He looked like a little boy… Tears welled up in her eyes as she still stood there gazing at him.

"Is it that bad now? Do I look a lot worse?"

Anna didn't have the heart to admit to that, so she quietly responded, "No, no, I'm just so happy to finally see you again. It's been so long. I was going to the coffee shop every single day for so many weeks, and finally it worked…"

"Come on in. Let's go to my room and talk then." Kevin looked tired.

Anna followed him, and just as they entered his room, Anna asked if his mom was at home. She knew the answer before he responded. Of course, his mom was at work.

Katie was at work as well, and Lauren was at the neighbor's house playing with her friend. His mom didn't want Kevin baby-sitting his little sister for long periods of time now because it made him really tired, and he needed to nap frequently in order to conserve his limited energy.

Anna listened, but all of it was hard to hear. It was so hard to understand and to accept. This situation was so different from what her Kevin, who now seemed a true adult, was experiencing while working at the best pizzeria in town.

"Anna, how about you? How have you been? How are things with you?" Kevin's eyes were bright, and it was obvious that he was interested in every word she was about to say.

So, Anna tried to fill him in on her life. She told him about school. She told him about the books she was reading, and she told him a little bit about her home life.

But when this Kevin asked her about her own Kevin, Anna was hesitant. She didn't know what to say. It was him after all but in a different reality, and he deserved to know. For some reason, though, it was so hard to talk about her Kevin's success while looking at this Kevin, who was now a lot sicker and weaker than even a few months ago. So, Anna told him about Kevin's job, but she tried to be as brief as possible. He probably felt it so he didn't push for any more information about her Kevin.

"How about Ann? How are things with her?" Anna was nervously looking at Kevin now.

"It's all over now. Completely over. If I used to see her at school, now I don't even get that now. I've been too sick to go to school for the last month, and she stopped talking to me completely after that. I tried calling and texting her a few times. I was hoping she would come and visit. I know that there's no more relationship, and the feelings on her side are over but…but I was hoping for the friendship.

She wasn't just my girlfriend. She was my best friend! We've known each other since Kindergarten. But she didn't respond to any of my calls or messages. I guess our friendship didn't mean as much to her as it did to me. It makes me very sad because I know I'll be gone soon, and I just wanted a little more time with her, you know…"

Anna had a really hard time controlling herself, trying not to cry. Everything Kevin was saying touched her heart, and she didn't understand how this other Ann could act like that. Technically it was her! It was her, but on this side of reality. The thoughts made Anna crazy, but at least it was easier to control her emotions now. She didn't want to cry in front of Kevin. It was hard for him as it was, and she didn't want to make it even harder.

"It's okay, Anna, really. It's okay…" she heard him whisper. How was he so strong in this moment? He was being strong for both of them.

"Kevin, I wanted to ask you something, but I didn't get a chance the last time I saw you."

"Yeah, go ahead."

"What happened to Ann's dad? Did her mom divorce him?" That question had been bugging her for the longest time, so she was really hoping to find something out.

"Oh, that's a weird story, and it happened not so long ago. I wasn't very close with Ann at the time, so I don't know all the details but, yes, they did divorce, and I know that Ann had a very hard time accepting it. She was his little girl all her life, and after the divorce, she stopped talking to him all together."

"Do you know why my…her parents divorced?"

"Not exactly. Ann told me once something like, 'He lost his mind. He's just crazy!' but, to be honest, I don't really know what that means."

"Oh I see…" Anna was hoping to find out more. She didn't have a dad in her own reality, and she really wanted to find out about Ann's dad. Not that it mattered, but she just wanted to, that's all.

Kevin saw her disappointment, so he offered to find out more.

"Can you?" Anna said, getting a little excited.

"To be honest, I don't know, but I can definitely try."

"That would be amazing. Can you also find out where he lives?"

"Are you going to go see him?" Anna heard surprise in his voice.

"I don't know…," and that was true. Anna really didn't know what she would do with the information.

"Are you hungry?" Kevin changed the subject while suddenly touching her hand.

Anna felt a shock go through her body. It was such a gentle touch, but it felt right, like it was her Kevin touching her even if that wasn't exactly the case…

"Actually, I am hungry. No, I am starving! Do you have anything to eat?" Anna was smiling at him now.

"We could go and check in the kitchen. Mom always leaves something for us. I'm sure we could find something."

They went to the kitchen and found snacks. They also talked more, and it felt so good talking to this Kevin. She almost felt like she was compensating for having missed out with her own Kevin for the last two months but, once again, she knew it wasn't really the case.

It was getting dark outside, and Anna told Kevin that it was probably time for her to go back. She also told him about the strange time difference. He was fascinated by that.

"You mean you were gone in your reality for a whole two days while you only spent like an hour here with me?!" Kevin couldn't believe it.

"Yes! Isn't that something?"

"Wow, that's so strange. But how?"

"Kevin, I don't know. I don't know how this whole thing works, but it still happens, and all I can do is accept it as it is."

"Then you need to hurry up. You spent like two hours here with me. Let me walk you back to the coffee shop. Was it the same day there when you left?"

"I think so. It was Friday afternoon when I left, so I'm hoping to make it to school by Monday morning."

"I sure hope you're going to make it. Let's go. Are you ready?"

Anna was ready, but she wasn't so sure about Kevin.

"Kevin, are you sure you can walk that far?" She looked at him with concern.

"Yeah, totally. Don't worry about me. Walks and fresh air are good for me anyway."

They walked to the coffee shop slowly, enjoying each other and enjoying the warm evening.

When they were about half way there, Kevin gently touched her hand again, just like he had done at his house. Kevin wanted to hold her hand, and Anna didn't say no. So, they kept walking hand in hand. By this point, however, they both were quiet and they didn't feel like they needed to talk anymore. Everything felt just right.

As they were standing by the coffee shop, Kevin looked Anna straight in the eyes and asked, "Will you come again?" There was so much hope in his eyes. It was hard to handle.

"I promise that I will try."

"I don't know how much time I have left."

"Oh Kevin, please don't say that."

"But it's true, though…I just hope I get to see you at least one more time."

Anna stood there, still holding his hand, not able say a word. *What do you say in a moment like this? What do you say?!*

Instead of initially speaking, Anna leaned closer and kissed Kevin on his cheek. Then she whispered in his ear, "I will do everything I can. Just wait for me, please. Promise me you're going to wait for me to come again."

"I promise."

Then Kevin opened the door, and Anna walked into the coffee shop. She was at home again, exhausted, hungry, and very sad…

Eighteen

Anna was standing in the coffee shop trying to understand what day and time it was. She had left her reality on Friday afternoon, and she was hoping to come back by Monday at school time.

But at the moment, it was hard to concentrate. Her head was pounding, and she felt very weak, hungry, and thirsty. Anna saw Robin behind the counter, so she went straight to her.

"Hi, Robin, can I please have some iced water? I'm so thirsty that I feel like I'm going to die."

"Of course. How was school today?" Robin was smiling in her friendly way.

"School? Oh, it was okay. Mondays are always rough." Anna responded.

"I'm sorry yesterday was rough. Was today any better?" Robin was waiting for her response, but Anna felt shocked.

So, it's not even Monday afternoon, it's Tuesday afternoon? Goodness! I spent like three hours on the other side. How can that be?

But by now Anna was learning just to accept things the way they were without trying to find logic. What happened, happened.

"Yeah, today was much better!"

"I'm glad to hear that. Here's your iced water. Are you going to stay here for the rest of the afternoon?" Once again, Robin was cheerful and friendly with her, unlike some of the other workers who frequently made her feel unwelcome here.

"No, I think I'm gonna head home now. Thanks for the water."

"No problem. See you around, Anna!"

Anna stepped outside, and the cool air made her feel a little better. Her head was still pounding, but it was easing up slightly.

Anna started walking home, still not able to organize her thoughts. It was too much to think about: Her time on the other side with Kevin. Kevin's condition getting obviously worse, and her desire to help him. Thoughts about Ann's dad and her desire to find him. And, of course, she was freaking out about being gone from her reality for so long.

The last time it had happened, it wasn't pretty with her Kevin. They had gotten into a big argument, and she feared that it was going to be even worse this time around. Her Kevin didn't believe her stories and, to be honest, she didn't blame him. Sometimes she questioned her sanity as well...

Anna checked her phone, but the battery was dead, so she sped up even more despite feeling exhausted. Once at home, Anna went straight to her room, plugged in her phone, and collapsed on her bed. While she was waiting for her phone to turn on, she thought of her mom sadly.

Has Mom been here at all? Did she even notice me being gone? Does she care about that stuff, or would she just prefer for me to disappear for good?

Finally her phone had charged enough to be turned on, and Anna shakily opened her text messages. There were a few from Kevin but not as many as she expected. She read the last one.

So srry, my boss asked me 2 work all 2day n I couldn't say no, so Ill miss school again. promise to make it up 2 u. Can we please meet 2nite? Can I come over? will bring pizza. Hope u r not too mad @ me. Please text me back when you can. IM SRRY!

Anna was relieved. Kevin wasn't mad at her. He was actually sorry himself. Well, that was just convenient.

But what happened, though? Anna thought as she was scrolling back to read his previous text messages. After a few minutes, it all made sense.

Kevin had worked Friday after school like he always did lately. Then he had worked both Saturday and Sunday, like he usually did as well, but his boss had asked him to stay for a few extra hours both days because they were very short-staffed.

By Sunday evening, Kevin felt guilty because Anna and Kevin had been planning to spend some time together. He assumed that she wasn't responding because she was mad at him.

On Monday, Kevin didn't come to school because his sister Lauren had a seizure episode again, and someone needed to stay home with her. Kevin ended up missing both school and work on Monday. He was apologizing to Anna again, but he also said in his text message that he knew how much she loved Lauren so he hoped that Anna wasn't too mad at him.

Everything made sense now. Kevin had had a rough weekend, but it all turned out to be very convenient for Anna. Now she wouldn't have to explain to him where she had been for the last three days. But, oh boy, how guilty it made her feel! Especially since little Lauren was sick again…

Anna thought for a second and then texted Kevin.

Can't wait 2 c u 2nite. Im sorry I was mad @ u. I was wrong. I understand u had 2 work n u had 2 watch Lauren. Im sorry I didnt respond earlier, but you know me - sometimes I just need a little time. Hows Lauren now? I hope shes better. Anyway, I'll see u tonight.

Anna pressed the send button on her phone, and then she curled up under her blanket. She felt exhausted but peaceful and ready to catch up on some sleep. She had a few hours before Kevin would come with his pizza.

Pizza…Food sounds so good now, but sleep first…

Nineteen

"Kevin, no, please don't go, please! Don't leave me here alone! Kevin, please…" Anna was crying by now, but he wasn't listening. He was walking away from her without even looking back. She thought her heart would stop, seeing him leave her. She loved him too much to let him go.

"Kevin!" she was trying to scream but her voice froze. Nothing came out no matter how hard she tried to scream. Then, suddenly, he stopped, turned around, looked her straight in the eyes and said quietly, "I'm not leaving you. You're the one who left me. It's you—it's all your fault. You lied to me. You're the one who ruined everything we had."

And then he was gone. Anna was all alone in the forest. It was getting darker and colder. Anna was scared, and she was hurt from his words. But he was right. She was the one who had left him. She was the one keeping secrets and disappearing. He had every right to blame her. Her heart was pounding. It was pounding so hard that she heard every sound it made, and it was getting louder and louder.

"Anna, are you home?!" Anna opened her eyes and sat up in the bed. She was at home, and it was getting dark outside. She wasn't in the forest. It had just been a dream.

"Anna, are you there?" Anna heard repeated knocks on the door again, and she recognized Kevin's voice.

She quickly got up and went to open the door.

"Hey, come on in."

"Are you okay in here? I was knocking on the door for like five minutes not knowing what to think. I thought you weren't mad at me anymore."

"I'm not mad. I was just sleeping."

"You don't sleep during the day." Kevin looked at her with a surprise.

"I know I don't, but today I did. I was so tired. And my head is killing me now." Anna felt like her whole body ached. She couldn't ever remember feeling so terrible before.

"You look like you're getting sick. Have you been feeling like this for a while?" There was concern in Kevin's voice.

"No, just today. You brought pizza? I'm so hungry!" Anna was more than hungry. She felt starving, like she hadn't had food for days.

"Oh yes, it's your favorite. Still warm." Kevin smiled at her.

"You're the best, you know that?!" Anna hugged him and gave him a quick kiss on his cheek.

"I'm starting to forget. And hey, is that all I get for being the best?" Kevin's smile got broader.

"That's all you get for now. Let me eat before I die. You want some tea or coffee? I think that's all we've got."

"No, I'm good. I ate at work not that long ago."

Anna made herself a cup of coffee, and she ate two slices of pizza while waiting for her coffee. Then she finally sat and slowed down.

"You should chew your food before you swallow it, you know. Just in case you forgot," said Kevin, tongue in cheek.

"Oh, you, just shut up." Anna wanted to throw something at him, but there was nothing soft around her.

"Jeez, you look like you didn't eat for a week!"

"Maybe I didn't?!"

"You're right. Anyway, tell me about school. How was it today?" asked Kevin.

"It was fine, nothing special. How was work, and how is Lauren doing?" Anna wanted to change the subject because she didn't want him to find out that she missed two days of school as well.

"Work is great. Lauren was home yesterday. She had a seizure in the early morning, and you know how weak she gets after she gets one of those. But she was better throughout the day, and she was able to go to school today."

"I'm glad to hear she's doing better."

"She said to tell you that she misses you. She wants you to come over. You think you could come visit her this week?"

"Well, you work every day. I don't wanna be there without you. I'll come whenever you have a day off."

"Okay, I'll let you know. I should have next week's schedule tomorrow. You feel better now after you ate this whole pizza on your own?" Kevin was smiling again.

"I didn't eat this whole pizza! You ate half of it." Anna was defensive. She always was when it came to food and weight. She was a typical teenager after all.

"Oh c'mon, I ate one little slice."

"You know I will hurt you if you say that one more time." Anna was only half joking.

"It's okay, Anna, really, one medium pizza is not so bad actually. It could have been large, you know." Kevin was obviously enjoying himself.

"You say one more word, and I promise I will hurt you!"

"You wanna go for a walk? Or watch a movie? Oh, and, by the way, who promised me more of something nice? I fed you, and you're just threatening to hurt me. How *not* nice of you!"

Anna went around the table to get closer to Kevin. Then she sat on his lap and wrapped her hands around his neck. She loved this boy so much; he was the best thing that had ever happened to her. But he sure knew how to make her mad!

"Kevin?" Anna whispered quietly in his ear.

"Yes?" his voice was so soft, and so were his lips.

"You know what I wanna do?"

"What's that?"

"I wanna…," Anna paused for emphasis, "watch a movie." She burst out laughing right in his ear.

"You're so silly! Don't laugh in my ear! That's too loud!" but Kevin was laughing too, though.

Anna and Kevin had so much fun together. They could spend hours enjoying each other's company, and they never got bored.

"Movie night it is!" said Kevin.

And Anna just felt so happy to be back.

Twenty

Anna and Kevin watched a movie while laying on the floor. They brought a blanket to lay on, and they found a few snacks in the kitchen.

It was getting late, but both of them didn't care. Anna never had to explain herself to her mom. She did wonder if her mom would show up tonight, and she wondered if her mom had noticed that she hadn't been home for a few days and nights. Anna doubted it, however.

As for Kevin, he was working now, and his mom had gotten used to him being gone almost always between school and work.

The movie was a beautiful love story. It was happy and sad at the same time. At least that's how Anna felt. While watching the story unfold, she was also thinking about love. She wondered if love could bring pure happiness to people.

Is it ever just happiness?

The more Anna thought about it, the more she was leaning toward thinking that life was never just like that. Love was way more complicated than that.

When the movie was over, Anna realized that she had tears in her eyes. She blinked and then wiped her face with her hands.

"Are you crying?" Kevin's voice was soft.

"Uh no, I'm not." Anna didn't want to admit that she had been crying over the movie. She was tougher than that. Right?

"It's okay to cry. I feel sad too. I actually enjoyed this movie. And I enjoyed finally spending time with you. I missed you these last couple of days. I missed seeing you and missed your texts." Anna looked at Kevin and noticed that he seemed a little sad.

"I missed you too," Anna whispered. Then she leaned closer and kissed his soft lips, which were warm and tasted like chocolate. That made her smile.

"Did you just eat the last piece of chocolate?"

"What chocolate?" Kevin looked innocent.

"You know what chocolate. You're terrible. You're addicted to chocolate!" Anna was laughing now.

"No, I'm not. I eat it because you don't like it."

"Oh, so you're doing me a favor? I don't eat it because I don't wanna get fat."

"You're not going to get fat. You look beautiful." Kevin looked at her with admiration. She knew that very well just by glancing at him. She loved it when he looked at her this way. It made her feel special.

"Kevin?" Anna got very quiet all of a sudden.

"Yes?"

"What do you think is going to happen in the next year? In the next five or ten years?" Anna looked him straight in the eyes.

"What do you mean?"

"I mean you and me. What do you think is gonna happen to us?"

"We're going to get married! What else?" Kevin was looking at her like he was explaining to her something as simple as how a vacuum worked. But to Anna, it wasn't that simple. She had never really thought about the future in that way. And now everything was getting very complicated with the other side and all.

"What? Why are you looking at me like this? You don't wanna marry me?" Kevin was smiling.

"Is that a proposal?" Anna started laughing.

Anna didn't want to continue talking about the topic. It made her uncomfortable. She wondered why she had asked him the question in the first place. There was too much she felt she couldn't tell him right now. She just wanted everything to remain perfect between them. Even if it meant keeping secrets from Kevin and not talking about the other side.

This time it was Kevin leaning closer and kissing her. She loved every second of it. He was a good kisser as far she knew, anyway, because he was the only boy who kissed her like this.

"You're so silly, Anna."

"I love you, Kevin," she whispered in his ear.

"I know. I love you, too."

Twenty-One

It was mid-June, and Anna was enjoying her summer break. She never was a big fan of school, but at the same time, she didn't mind being with other kids her age. Also, going to school meant seeing Kevin, especially after he started working. Anna missed all their time together, so she was looking forward to the summer break, not realizing that wasn't going to happen this summer as Kevin would begin working at the pizzeria full time the day their summer break began.

Anna was disappointed at first, but she also understood and accepted Kevin's decision. She told herself numerous times that he needed to work to help his family, and she would do the same the day she turned sixteen. But for now she had nothing else to do but wait for that day to come.

That and the coffee shop. Anna started spending even more time there. She would bring a book and sometimes a little snack from home, and she would just sit in her little corner and wait. It wasn't hard because Anna liked the shop's atmosphere, and she started enjoying all the books she was reading. She realized that books could make her feel happy, and they also could make her feel sad. They were little doors into other people's lives, even if those lives were imaginary.

Finally, in mid-July, it happened again. Anna left her apartment in the morning as always, headed to the shop, and settled in once there. It felt like an ordinary day. She had enough money to order an iced tea, and after the tea was almost gone and she was about one third of the way deep into her new book, she heard their familiar voices again.

Anna looked up and sure enough, there they were—her gorgeous mom and Ann. They both looked tanned, like they had just come back from an exotic vacation, and they were wearing bright, short dresses and big glasses. They looked well-rested and happy.

Anna watched them both ordering iced drinks to go and leaving the coffee shop as soon as their drinks were made. Without even a slight hesitation, Anna grabbed her things and followed the two outside making it just in time to get the door while Ann was still touching it. And just like that Anna was on the other side once again. It felt so strange and so good at the same time. Anna almost felt like she was breaking some rules, like she was doing something she shouldn't be doing but, oh boy, it felt so good for unknown-even-to-her reasons.

Anna started walking down the street, knowing very well where she was headed. The closer she got to Kevin's house, the more anxious she felt.

What will I see there? How is he doing? Is he worse? That particular thought definitely scared her.

Will he be happy to see me again? What will we talk about? Will it feel awkward or not? Anna had many more questions, and all were racing in her head.

Before she knew it, Anna was standing in front of Kevin's house—too nervous to knock on the door, just as she had been the last time she was here. Every time Anna started to knock, she got too scared again, so she waited and waited. Before Anna had a chance to decide what to do, the front door opened wide and she saw Kevin's mom, Elizabeth, standing right in front of her.

"Ann? I thought I heard something at the door so I decided to check. Are you here to visit Kevin? Come on in. I'm sure he'll be so very happy to see you. He's missed you a lot. Especially lately…"

"Hi. Um…I missed him as well." Anna hesitated because she didn't know how much Elizabeth might know. Did Elizabeth know who Anna really was, or did she only believe that she was the other Ann, Kevin's childhood friend and ex-girlfriend? Anna decided to say as little as possible until she talked to Kevin.

"You could have come more frequently, you know." Anna heard an edge in Elizabeth's voice and concluded that Elizabeth thought that she was Ann and didn't know anything about Anna's mysterious existence.

"I'm sorry. Can I see him? How's he doing?"

"Oh Ann…Kevin is getting weaker and weaker every day. I don't know how much longer he has. He can barely walk now, and he's very sad. He won't talk to me about it, so I don't even know what's bothering him the most. But if you ask me, it has something to do with you. I know he misses you every day."

"Mom? Who are you talking to?" Anna heard Kevin's voice from one of the rooms.

"Ann, I'm glad you came. Please talk to him. I hope it will cheer him up a little bit. I'm sorry if I sounded irritated with you just now. I shouldn't blame you for anything. This is not your fault." Elizabeth was smiling, but there was so much sadness and pain in that smile that it almost brought tears into Anna's eyes.

Anna hesitated, and then she took a deep breath and said, "I'm so sorry for everything. I am, really. Please forgive me."

Then Anna leaned closer and hugged Elizabeth. It simply didn't matter in this second that she wasn't that Ann who had broken up with Kevin or that she wasn't the one who had caused all his sufferings. In Elizabeth's eyes, Anna was exactly that person, and Elizabeth was still so kind to her.

Anna felt even more respect for this woman now. She also wanted to tell Elizabeth everything. She didn't want Elizabeth to judge her for breaking up with Kevin. Anna wanted her to know that it wasn't her. She wanted Elizabeth to know that she loved Kevin in her reality, and she cared deeply for this Kevin as well. Maybe she even loved both of them…it was too complicated to understand.

That's the thing—it was too complicated to understand, and also it was too complicated to explain to another person. So, Anna just kept everything as it was.

"I'll go see him now. Thank you for letting me." Anna smiled and headed toward Kevin's bedroom.

Anna didn't know what she would see once she opened the door, but she felt that she was ready for anything, no matter how bad or how sad. She was doing this for Kevin.

Twenty-Two

"Anna…" There was definite surprise in Kevin's voice.

"Hey, there." Anna swallowed her tears when she saw him. He looked so much worse. He looked so vulnerable, so small.

"You came" was all he said.

"Of course, I did. I promised you I would."

"Well, come here. Come sit with me and tell me everything."

Anna came closer, put her backpack on the floor, and sat down on the edge of Kevin's bed next to where he was laying. He was covered with a blanket, and it was only his skinny arms and his bold pale head that she saw, but it was enough to paint a picture of Kevin's disease progression. It had to be bad. Anna didn't expect to see what she was seeing. It was happening too soon. It was too much for her to handle. She didn't know what to say, but she felt a desperate urge to fill the silence.

"Your mom doesn't know who I am, does she?" Anna blurted out because she truly didn't know what else to say. Somehow talking about her summer break and Kevin's full time job didn't feel right.

"No. I didn't tell her. Oh boy, was she not nice to you?!"

"Oh, no! Absolutely not! Your mom's a very sweet women. You're blessed to have her." And Anna meant it. She had always wanted her own mom to be more like Elizabeth—caring, loving, hard-working, and dedicated to her children.

"Oh, good. I got nervous for a second. She's mad at Ann for breaking up with me, but knowing my mom, she would forgive her the second she sees her. She's probably so excited that my best friend and the love of my life finally came to see me today."

Anna felt awkward. She didn't know what to say. Sure, Ann was the 'love of Kevin's life,' but today Ann wasn't here with him. It was her, Anna, sitting in front of Kevin, and of course, she wasn't the 'love of his life.' What Kevin said wasn't very logical. But so what? Nothing was very logical about this whole situation! And Anna knew better than anyone else that she just had to accept things as they were without constantly trying to explain everything.

Before Anna had a chance to say something else, Kevin's face lit up with a huge smile as he exclaimed, "Anna! I totally forgot! Guess what?!"

Anna didn't know what to think.

"What?" she asked carefully.

"I found out where your dad lives! I mean Ann's dad. Or does it mean he's your dad as well? Sorry, it's so complicated. I guess I didn't think about that little detail."

"You did? Where does he live?" Anna didn't know if Ann's dad was her dad as well in her reality.

In fact, Anna didn't know much about her own dad, period. Anna remembered a male character from her early childhood back when her mom used to be normal and happy, but she wasn't totally sure if he was her biological dad. Talking about that with her mom was unbearable. The older Anna got, the worse her mom became, and normal conversations were not part of their lives, or co-existence, if anyone were to ask Anna.

And now Kevin was telling Anna about Ann's dad, so she was going to take every chance she had without thinking too hard about whose dad the man really was. She was dying to belong and to have family.

"He lives not too far from here. It would take you maybe an hour to walk...if you walk fast."

"You have his address and everything?"

"I sure do!" Kevin was smiling. It was obvious that he was very pleased at seeing how happy and excited Anna was.

"What're you going to do? Will you go see him?" Kevin's question brought Anna back to reality.

"I don't know. Should I?" Anna was looking at Kevin and hoping that he would tell her to go see Ann's dad. She really wanted to, but she needed someone's support. She simply needed someone to tell her that she wasn't completely crazy.

"Why not?" was all he said, but even that was enough for Anna.

"Okay. Then I'll go and see him. I need to do it before I get too scared and change my mind. I have no idea what I'm going to tell him or if he will even look at me. I don't know if I should pretend that I am Ann or if I should just tell him everything as it is...All I know is that I really want to meet him! And then we'll see what happens."

"Here's the address then. It's seven o'clock now. He should be at home from work. You should hurry up before it's too chilly and dark outside."

"Okay then." Anna stood up, feeling all kinds of emotions rushing through her.

"Anna?" Kevin's voice was small, like he was hesitating to speak up.

"Yes?"

"Are you going to come back after you see him?" There was so much hope in Kevin's eyes.

"Of course, I'll come back! I'm not done talking to you. We need to catch up on everything. But I really wanna see Ann's dad today before I change my mind. Plus, we'll need to work out a plan to get me back to my reality. I have no idea how we're going to do that. It seems like it's only you who can get me back home. I might be wrong, though, but that's just how it was the last couple times."

"Don't worry. We're going to get you there. Now, go and see him. Good luck. And don't worry. I'm sure it'll be okay. Steve's very nice."

"Steve?"

"Yes, Steve is his name."

Steve was the name of the guy Anna slightly remembered from early childhood, which gave her a hope that Steve was her dad in her reality as well. She just had to be brave enough to go and find out.

"Thanks, Kevin. You'll have to tell me how you managed to get his address when I come back."

"And you will have to tell me how everything goes!"

Anna looked at Kevin one more time, smiled, and went toward the door. At the door, she stopped for a second to wave goodbye, and them she was gone. She was on her way to see Steve. Anna just hoped that she wasn't making a mistake.

Twenty-Three

*A*nna walked as fast as she could. She was clutching a piece of paper with Steve's address in her right hand, and she would peer down at it from time to time even though she had already memorized his address by now. The piece of paper was more like a confirmation that Steve was a real person, and it was happening now. She really was on her way to meet him.

About an hour and fifteen minutes later, Anna stood in front of the house. She looked at the piece of paper one last time just to confirm that she was at the right place.

This is it. I did it. Now, I just need to be brave enough to go and knock on the door.

But that was easier to think than to do. Anna felt a rush of emotions flowing through her again. It was Anna's sincere desire to meet Steve and to talk to him, but she was very anxious about actually doing it.

What if he's not alone? I never asked Kevin if Steve got married again. What if there is a whole new family in his house? They may not necessarily be happy to see me. Oh, my goodness, why didn't I ask Kevin about that? Maybe he's not married but is dating someone.

That would be just as terrible as him being married. Well, maybe not as terrible but still very terrible. Oh, whatever, Anna! Just do it! Just go and knock on the door! What's the worst thing that could possibly happen? He will get mad and yell at you for you to get out. That's not so bad, you can handle that.

And Anna did it. She went up to the front door and knocked. There were lights on upstairs and a parked car in the driveway, so she knew someone was home. Then, after she knocked on the door and heard someone's steps approaching, she realized that there was no going back. For a second, though, she wanted to run away and pretend that it had never happened.

It's not like Steve will run after me, right?

But Anna didn't run. She stood stalwartly there waiting as someone was fumbling with the lock on the door, and as she was calling for all the braveness to be within her in that moment because, God knew, she needed all of it.

The door opened, and she saw Steve. Of course, Anna wasn't completely sure it was him, but she assumed. His face was hard to read. Was he mad because someone was disturbing his evening? Or was he just a little irritated? Or was it simply shock on his face?

The two stood silently for a moment. It seemed an eternity to Anna. They were staring at each other as if their minds were working hard trying to figure out what to do next.

Finally, Steve spoke, "Ann?"

Was he shocked that Anna...Ann had finally come to talk to him as she had been very mad at him after the divorce? Or did he see that it wasn't really Ann but someone that looked very much alike, yet a different person? Anna didn't know.

"Hi. Can I come in?"

Anna wasn't planning on spilling the story to him while she was still standing outside. The conversation she was about to have with Steve wasn't exactly a five-minute long, easy conversation, but asking to come in inside was a brave move as well. She didn't know him. Ann's mom and Steve had divorced because 'he was crazy' in Ann's own words.

Will I be safe in this man's house? How crazy is he? And crazy in what way? Anna didn't know.

I guess I'll find out soon.

Twenty-Four

They were sitting at the kitchen table, chewing halfheartedly on peanuts that just happened to be there in a bowl, and talking. Steve didn't look crazy to Anna thus far. He looked like a normal person—with clean clothing, a shaved face, and nice hair. He was calm and knew how to listen.

"So…you're telling me that you're Anna, and you remember me from your childhood, but you live on the other side?" Steve's voice remained calm after Anna had finished telling him her story.

"Yes! But you don't believe me, do you?" Anna knew that the chances of him believing her were slim.

"And every time you came to this side it has happened when Ann and her mom have been at the coffee shop?"

He was still interested. That was a good sign.

"Yes, it seems like that's exactly how it works."

"And Kevin was the person who's helped you to get back?" Steve looked like he was concentrating and trying to figure something out.

"Yes."

"Tell me more about your life. Tell me about your mom."

Anna hesitated, but she felt like she could trust Steve. She wasn't ashamed to talk about her life in front of him. So, Anna told him about her early childhood memories. She didn't have many, but they were happy memories.

Then Anna told him how things changed and how her mom was doing now. It was painful for Anna to talk about her mom and her alcohol issues, but she also saw that it was painful for Steve to listen. She told Steve her story in a matter of fact tone, not complaining once.

Anna didn't want Steve to feel bad for her; it wasn't the point of their meeting. She also told him about her Kevin and how she felt about the young man. Anna was happy to have Kevin in her life, but she didn't know how to handle the whole situation with the other side as her Kevin simply didn't believe her.

"This is hard to hear. But I totally understand how you feel, Anna." Steve's voice was so quiet that Anna felt she didn't catch the whole phrase.

"Excuse me?" Anna wanted him to repeat what he just said, but Steve remained quiet and was just looking at his hands.

"Steve? What did you say? I didn't hear you."

Steve looked startled, like he had totally forgotten for a moment that Anna was still sitting next to him.

"Oh, I'm sorry. By the way, are you hungry? When was the last time you ate?"

Anna was surprised by his question. Food had been the last thing on her mind. But now, as Steve mentioned it, she realized that she was starving. She was shy to admit it, but Steve recognized immediately that she was hungry, so he didn't wait for her answer.

"I have some take out leftovers from last night. It's nothing fancy, but it's better than nothing. Let me heat it up really quick. Also, I have chips and grapes."

Steve wasn't asking her anymore. He just set the food in front of Anna, and he started eating as well so she didn't feel uncomfortable. The food tasted good.

I hope I'm not going to die from this! It was a silly thought, but it made Anna smile.

Why can't I think of something more serious?

"What are you smiling about?" Steve asked suddenly.

"I was hoping that eating food on this side will not make me die!" Anna burst out laughing.

Steve joined her, and then they both were laughing to the point of having tears in their eyes. The second they stopped laughing, though, they burst into another round until Anna was holding her stomach.

"Stop it! I can't laugh anymore! My stomach hurts!"

Steve calmed down a bit. He was quiet for a moment, so Anna started eating grapes again. Then he very seriously, like the whole hysteria had never happened, stated, "I am so proud of you, Anna! You are so much braver than I am."

Anna looked at him while trying to understand what he was talking about. She kept looking at him, and it was apparent that she was waiting for him to explain himself, but Steve didn't hurry himself to make things simple and easy for her to understand.

"Do you know why I got divorced?" were Steve's next words.

"No." Anna stopped eating, all ears.

"But what do you know about me and Ann's mom getting divorced? I'm sure Kevin told you a thing or two about me and our divorce."

Anna hesitated. She didn't necessarily want to tell Steve that she had heard he was crazy, and that was why they had gotten divorced.

"I don't know much, really. I just wanted to find you, and Kevin was so good about helping me with that. But you tell me. What happened?" However, Steve wasn't ready to give up on learning what Anna knew.

"Did Kevin tell you that I was crazy?" Steve looked directly at her, and Anna didn't have the nerve to lie to him.

"He did." She said it quietly, but she kept looking at him. She didn't think Steve was crazy, and she hoped that Steve saw that.

"Well, maybe they're right. Maybe I am crazy. I'll tell you a story, and you be my judge here." Anna didn't say anything, but she was ready to listen. Steve was quiet for a few moments, as if gathering his thoughts, and then he started talking again.

"The first time it happened, I really thought I was losing my mind. I didn't tell anyone and tried to forget about it. I tried to pretend like it never happened. That wasn't easy, but I managed.

But then it happened again and again, and I had to tell someone. So, I told Ann's mom. Maria didn't believe me. Of course, who would? And I don't blame her. I really don't.

I tried to show her, but it never worked. She never saw what I saw...I saw you, Anna. At the coffee shop.

I saw you there many times, and I didn't understand what exactly it meant, but I knew that you were my daughter but a different version of her. Not as happy, often sad and hungry looking.

But I never had the courage to come forward and talk to you. I was never brave enough, like you were. I never tried to go to the other side, as you call it. I wasn't even sure if it existed. But I knew for sure that you existed and…and it was all too confusing and too hard to understand.

Moreover, it seemed insane to try and explain to someone who wasn't very open-minded about the whole 'different version of our daughter' thing. Oh, Anna, I feel so guilty…I wanted to save my marriage, but we had more and more issues with time.

I wanted to focus on my real life. But who was I to say which version of you was real and which one wasn't? I am so mad at myself for giving up, for stopping going back to the coffee shop.

As you can see, it didn't help my marriage. It's over. Both my wife…my ex-wife and Ann think that I'm crazy, and I even almost let them convince myself that I was crazy…Ann won't even talk to me since the divorce.

But here you are, telling me about the other side, your life there, your mom Maria, and your travels back and forth. Not being ashamed of yourself and simply trusting me with your story. I am so very proud of you. I wish I was more like you."

Anna couldn't believe the words she was hearing. Was Steve for real? Or was he a little crazy, just like they claimed he was? But who was she kidding? She knew better than anyone that the other side was real!

Of course, Steve was serious and, of course, he was telling her the truth. Anna was his daughter after all, and maybe the whole thing was in their genes—even if it was a crazy gene causing all this to happen. At the moment, however, Anna didn't care. She came closer and hugged Steve.

"Thank you for sharing your story with me, Steve. I'm so sorry things turned out the way they did for you. But I'm so glad I've found you. I know for sure that all this happened for a reason. I think I am beginning to understand, but I can't be certain for sure. Not just yet. I have to ask you, though—will you help me with something?"

"Whatever it is, Anna, I promise to help you." She heard him respond, and that's all she needed to hear.

Twenty-Five

*A*nna woke to the smell of eggs, bacon, and freshly brewed coffee. That was unusual. Her apartment was always cold and almost never smelled like breakfast in the mornings. But today, Anna didn't wake up in her own home. Steve had offered for her to stay at his house for the night and had gotten everything ready for her in his guest bedroom.

Anna didn't feel very comfortable, but she simply didn't have a choice. She had needed to spend the night somewhere, and Steve was her father after all. Of course, it was the other Steve, the one on the other side, but what difference did it make in a situation like this one?

They had spent the rest of the evening talking and sharing memories with each other, and then they had come up with a plan. Neither of them was completely sure it would work, but after talking through it several more times, they had agreed that it was the right thing to do. Now, laying in the bed and thinking about last evening, Anna started questioning herself again.

Is this the right thing to do? How will I explain everything to my Kevin? Will he believe me and will he accept my decision? Will he understand why I'm doing this? Will he understand how much I actually love him?

Anna didn't have answers to her questions. She just had a feeling that her plan was the right thing to do, and she was going to trust herself about it. And now, having Steve on her side, she knew just how to make the whole thing work.

Ten minutes later, she met Steve in the kitchen.

"Good morning. The entire house smells delicious," Anna said.

"Ready for breakfast? It's not exactly a five star restaurant, but it's the best I can do."

"I'm sure it's worth five stars. It smells and looks very good." Anna smiled while looking at the plate he sat in front of her. She was also thinking about Ann and how she probably had a breakfast like this one every morning.

Is she grateful for everything she has? Or does she take it all for granted? But then, Anna decided not to think about it anymore. It was Ann's business after all.

"So are we still on?" Steve asked, interrupting Anna's thoughts.

"Yes."

"Okay, then let's hurry up and go. I need to be at work in forty minutes. I'll drop you off at Kevin's and will pick you up in the evening around five or so. You guys talk about the plan and make sure he's okay with it too."

"I hope he'll like it," Anna voiced on her way to the sink to wash her plate.

"Just put it in the dishwasher."

"Huh?" Anna didn't have a dishwasher in her apartment, so washing dishes was an old habit.

"Just put your plate in the dishwasher," Steve repeated, and his raised eyebrows showed that he was surprised by Anna's reaction.

"Oh, okay!"

And then they were on their way to Kevin's house. Both were quiet in the car, lost in their own thoughts. Neither of them was sure about the whole idea, but it did seem like a great one.

I guess we'll have to wait and see how it goes.

Twenty-Six

By eleven that morning, Anna and Kevin had caught up on their lives. Anna talked about her summer break and her Kevin's job as well as her own mom and her latest boyfriend who, despite being in his fifties, still didn't seem to know how to use the toilet or wash his hands properly without making the whole bathroom look like a total disaster.

Kevin talked about his sister Lauren and her progress at school and how his mom was so proud of her. And he talked about his latest appointments with the oncologist and his recent hospital stay. Kevin didn't look sad when he talked about his disease. It appeared like he had accepted his situation with grace.

Anna, on the other hand, was still trying to grasp the idea that Kevin, her Kevin, even if it was the one from the other side, was so seriously sick that he was basically slowly dying.

"Do you ever think about death?" asked Kevin.

Anna did think about death nowadays, but that thought process was new to her. She had never really thought about death before meeting this Kevin.

"Sometimes I guess I do," replied Anna, beginning to worry about this whole conversation and where it was heading.

"Would you be afraid to die?"

Kevin wasn't going to stop. Anna didn't want to talk about death. It wasn't an easy subject, especially with Kevin! But then she thought that he probably really wanted and even needed to talk to someone about the topic, and she was just the right person. She knew that it would be so much harder for Kevin to talk about death with his mom, for instance.

"I don't know, Kevin. I didn't necessarily think about it."

"Then think about it now. Just for a second. Just pretend that you have one more month to live. What do you feel? Are you scared?"

Anna felt goosebumps raise on her back. She wanted to change the subject again so badly, but she did what he asked her to do. She imagined for a minute and then she responded, "I don't know if I am scared, but I am sad. I wouldn't want to die.

I would be so sad to leave everyone behind. Even though I don't have that many people to leave behind. But still…I wanna grow older and see what's going to happen to people I know.

I don't wanna leave Kevin behind. I love him too much. What if nobody else ever loves him the way that I do?

I wouldn't even want to leave my mom behind. I still like to think that she cares about me.

And overall, it just would be so weird to be gone from this world while nothing else changes. I would be gone, but life would go on. The sun would rise every morning, and people will keep on with their lives…for them, it would be like nothing had changed…" Anna looked up and saw Kevin.

He was looking directly at her and listening very carefully.

"Maybe it's strange, but that's exactly how I feel. I don't wanna die because I know how hard it will be for my mom and my sisters.

Also, it's devastating to think about what you just said. Nothing will change for the rest of the world when I die. Nothing…"

Anna couldn't handle the conversation any longer. It was simply getting too heavy. She didn't want to cry in front of Kevin and make things even worse for him. She didn't want him comforting her when it was supposed to be the other way around. She needed to do something to stop this.

"Hey, are you hungry? It's lunch time."

"No, I'm not. I don't really get hungry nowadays. The nausea it too strong, and I can't seem to keep food down anyway."

"Oh…I'm sorry to hear that."

"That's okay, it's nothing new. But, hey, are you hungry?"

"I could eat ice cream! I really want some ice cream."

"I don't know if we have any. Would you mind going to the kitchen and checking the freezer?"

"Sure."

Anna didn't feel like eating ice cream, but she needed an excuse to politely stop the conversation. So, she went to the kitchen and opened the freezer looking for ice cream. Kevin was right—there was none. Anna didn't feel ready to go back to Kevin in case he wasn't finished talking about dying.

She yelled from the kitchen, "I don't see any. I'll go to the store and buy some. Okay? I saw a grocery store just a few blocks away from your house."

"Okay. I'm sorry we don't have any. Do you need money?" Kevin's voice was quiet, but she was able to understand.

"No, don't worry. I've got money!" yelled Anna back while stepping outside.

That was a lie. She didn't have any money with her, but she didn't care. She started walking toward the grocery store that she had seen on her way to Kevin's house this morning.

In a few minutes, Anna was standing in front of the freezers filled with a variety of ice creams.

Which one should I get? I don't really want any, but maybe Kevin will eat some. Maybe it will even help with the nausea. But which one does he like? Why didn't I ask him? Well…my Kevin loves the pistachio one, so I'll take my chances and get the pistachio.

Anna opened the freezer and grabbed the ice cream. It was so cold that she didn't know how she would do it. She couldn't hide the ice cold package under her T-shirt.

Anna kept walking between the aisles while pretending to look at food options. Meanwhile she was making a plan. She hated herself for doing this. She didn't even know why she was doing it. She suspected that it was all about getting an adrenaline rush, and she craved one at the moment.

Just don't get caught. Just don't get caught. You can be in a lot of trouble if you do. Don't get caught. Keep looking toward the exit and pretend that you're confident and have nothing to worry about.

Nothing to be scared of. It's okay. You've done it before a couple of times, and it was fine. It's just ice cream! Even if you get caught, pretend that you forgot to pay. That's it, go toward the exit. Almost there...

"Excuse me, miss!" Anna's heart sank. She turned around and saw a security officer.

"Are you talking to me?"

"Yes, I am talking to you. You need to come with me. Now."

"Why? I'm not going anywhere!" Anna was panicking.

They can't be so serious about stupid ice cream!

"Then we're going to wait here. The police are on their way."

"What? I forgot to pay for ice cream! Is that such a big deal?" Anna was almost yelling, but her own voice sounded strange to her, like it was someone's else.

"Ice cream is not such a big deal. But the other things that you stole before are a big deal." The security officer looked calm and confident. He looked like he knew what he was talking about. But what in the world was he talking about?

"What other things?" questioned Anna, becoming even more nervous. No, she was terrified!

"You know what other things you stole. We have everything recorded on camera. Or did you think that if you dress like a homeless person and change your hair a little bit, we're not going to notice you?"

Anna didn't know what to think. Her mind was racing. She couldn't even get offended by his comment about her looking like a homeless person.

What is going on here? Has Ann been stealing from this store, and now they think I am her? Crap. Things are about to turn very ugly.

Anna decided to be silent and not tell the security officer or the police officers anything, not even her name.

That's it. That's what I'm going to do. Deny everything and not reveal any information.

But things were worse than Anna thought. She didn't have to give them her name. They already had it.

Oh brother... I'm dead! Anna found that errant, dark thought funny. She was thinking about death after all!

Twenty-Seven

"Your mother is on her way, young lady. And I hope you're ashamed of yourself." The security officer's tone was harsh.

Anna sat in the small manager's office and trembled. She was so scared.

What's going to happen to me now? Will they know that I'm from the other side? If they won't, will I go to jail? If I tell them, will they think that I am crazy or even mentally unstable and ill? Anna didn't know which option was worse.

Anna just knew that she was in a bad situation, period. She was also terrified of meeting Ann's mom.

What is she going to say? She probably will see immediately that I'm not her daughter. The security officer was right—I look like a homeless person compared to the fancily dressed and tanned Ann.

Despite her panic, Anna kept thinking, and then she had an idea. It was the only chance she had. She wasn't sure that it would work, but she just had to try.

"Can you call my dad, please?" Anna voice was small as she was scared to say much of anything.

"We already called your mother, and she's coming."

"Well, she works across town, and it's going to take her over an hour to get here, even if the traffic's not bad. But my dad could be here in fifteen minutes."

Anna had no idea where Ann's mom or dad worked or how long it would take either of them to come to the store. She was simply taking her chances.

The officer looked at her for a long few seconds, like he was trying to decide if she was lying to him or not, and probably considering if he wanted to spend the next hour waiting in this tiny office.

"You've got his phone number?"

Anna exhaled. She hadn't realized she had been holding her breath. Now she realized that she had a chance, even if a very small one.

Anna spilled Steve's phone number to the officer and then said a little prayer in her head for Steve to answer the phone and to come rescue her.

Anna was so grateful this once for her freakishly good memory! She almost always remembered odd things such as birth dates of random people from history, a few addresses if they meant anything to her, and, of course, phone numbers. She had a whole phone book in her head. If she saw the number once, she knew it. Sometimes it came in handy…

And then Anna waited. And waited. Every minute felt like an hour to Anna.

Who will show up first? Ann's mom or Steve?

If Steve showed up first, Anna knew that she would be relieved. And ashamed. Very ashamed. She didn't know what she would tell him, but she was sure they could sort it out and move on.

If Ann's mom showed up first, however, Anna simply didn't know how things would turn out. She had no choice but wait.

Fifteen minutes later, the door opened, and Anna saw Steve. To say that Anna was relieved was a significant understatement.

Before Anna fully realized what she was doing, she was already on her feet, hugging Steve tightly and repeating, "Thank you for coming, I'll explain everything, I promise. But thank you so much…"

Twenty-Eight

For the next ten awkward minutes, Anna watched videos of Ann stealing from the store. Ann had stolen little things as well as more expensive items.

And Anna couldn't help but think, *Why does she do this? I'm sure her mom gives her enough money to buy all the things that she chose to steal. What is wrong with her?* But then again, Anna herself wasn't going to die without that ice cream today, and yet she attempted to leave the store without bothering to pay for it…

We both are just bad like that, rotten people. The idea made Anna very sad. She wanted to be better than that.

Sitting in the little office and watching the videos, Anna made herself a promise that she would never steal again.

Never. Never ever again in my life. It needs to stop. Even if I am dying from starvation, I will not steal again. I promise. I swear.

Anna looked at Steve. He appeared shocked and sad at the same time. It must have been very hard to watch his daughter and realize she was a thief. Especially as Ann likely had no good excuse for her actions.

Anna wanted to hug Steve and tell him that everything would be okay and promise him that she would never steal again. But

Steve was probably more concerned about his real daughter, Ann, not her.

Then Steve and the security officer stepped out of the room, and Anna was left all by herself with her thoughts.

What are they talking about? Will Steve tell the officer that I'm not actually his daughter? Will he tell him that I'm from the other side? Will he leave me in here to wait for Ann's mom to arrive?

Oh my goodness, what's taking them so long? My heart'll explode from worrying! And my bladder might explode, too, because I needed to pee like an hour ago when Kevin started talking about death.

Kevin! He must be worrying about me, not knowing what's taking me so long. He might think I got lost. Or worse! He might think that I couldn't handle our conversation and ran away! No, no, no...

"Are you ready to go?" That was Steve talking.

"Go? Go where?" Anna was so scared to find out that she almost burst into tears. "Home" was all Steve said.

"Home?" Anna was afraid that she hadn't heard correctly.

Steve just stood in the doorway and looked at her. But seeing that Anna wasn't moving, he encouraged her to move.

"Yes, home. We're going to meet your mother there, and we're going to have a very serious conversation. I hope you realize how much trouble you are in and how serious the consequences are going to be."

Consequences? Mother? We're going to meet my mother? Ann's mother? But why?

Then Anna looked at Steve again and saw him begging her with his eyes for her to hurry up.

Right! We need to get out of here before Ann's mom shows up! I'm so stupid!

Anna stood up, and they finally were on their way out. She had so many questions for Steve.

First of all, how did he convince the security officer to let me go? Second, where are we really going?

Anna hoped that they weren't going home to meet with "her mother" as had Steve claimed just a few moments ago.

And, of course, Anna wanted to talk to Steve about the whole stealing situation...

Only later did Anna realize that police had never showed up. She kept wondering if that was because the security officer had only been trying to scare her.

Twenty-Nine

Anna told Steve everything. She told him about every single time she had stolen something.

It started with stealing food at the grocery store. She was younger and couldn't understand completely how wrong it was. When her mom didn't show up at home for four days in a row and she had run out of food, however, she went to the store and stole some chips. Then she went there again and stole some more.

Anna always felt terrible afterwards and didn't steal anything again for a while. But then it happened again. And again.

One time it wasn't food, though. It was a little doll. Tiny, really. Anna saw it in the store and couldn't pass it. It looked so appealing, so cute. She didn't really have any toys to play with and that doll was too cute to leave her in the store.

By that time, Anna was already older and she knew very well that stealing was wrong and she could get into trouble by doing it. But she still came home with the doll. She was almost eleven then. The funny thing is, she never played with it. Every time she looked at the doll, she felt sick to her stomach. How pathetic…

And then it was a bracelet for Kevin. She wasn't proud of that one neither.

And, today, stupid ice cream…

Now Steve knew everything. Anna felt relieved after telling him. She didn't know why, but it felt good that there was someone who finally knew how bad she was.

"Oh, Anna, come here, sweetie. Let me hug you." Anna saw tears in Steve's eyes.

"Why are you saying this? Aren't you mad at me? Ashamed? Don't you feel disgusted about me and what I've done?"

"No, I don't." His hug was tight, and his tears were hot on Anna's neck.

"Steve? Are you okay?"

"I just feel so terrible that your life turned out the way it did—your childhood, I mean. Your life is still ahead of you, and you can do anything you want with it. And I'm sure you will make the right choices from now on. You're a bright young lady with a good heart."

Now Anna wanted to cry. She wasn't used to hearing things like that. It was only Kevin who had always been nice to her, but even that was different.

"Thank you," was all she said, and she felt like it was enough because Steve knew how she was feeling.

"Let me feed you now, and then I will have to deal with Ann and all the stealing she has been doing. I just can't believe it…"

Anna heard the change in his voice. It was no longer calm and understanding.

How is it different? We both were stealing, but Steve isn't so soft voiced when talking about Ann. His own daughter!

Steve started talking again, like he knew exactly what Anna had been thinking about.

"The thing is, that girl has everything she needs and everything she wants. She has money. Her mom spoils her like there's no tomorrow. I give them money as well. Ann gets most of it, even though she is refusing to even talk to me.

But that wasn't enough! She needed to steal! I hope Maria will take it seriously. Ann needs to have consequences for her actions."

"Steve, please don't jump to conclusions before you talk to Ann. She might have her own reasons. It might be her way of coping with the divorce. You never know. Try to talk to her and hear her out."

"Oh, I would love to talk to her! But she's too good to acknowledge my existence nowadays!"

Anna didn't know what to say to that. She just hoped that things between Steve and Ann could be worked out. He needed his daughter, and Ann needed her dad. Wasn't that just logical?

Thirty

Anna didn't want to tell Kevin about her stealing, but she had to explain to him why she had been gone for hours when she had only left to get some ice cream and then came back without any.

At first, Anna thought that she would come up with a story just for Kevin, but then she decided not to. She didn't want to be a thief and a liar. Being a thief was bad enough.

To Anna's surprise, Kevin didn't judge her. Or maybe he did, but he didn't show any judgment as she was telling him. Maybe he had more serious things on his mind, like dying in the near future. Anna didn't know, and she didn't ask. Their earlier conversation about dying had led her to attempt stealing the ice cream in the first place.

Instead, they just spent the rest of the afternoon together: talking, sharing memories, finding common things in their lives, and looking through old pictures.

Anna was fascinated by Kevin's stories, his feelings toward Ann, and his inability to be mad at her even after she had broken up with him.

Anna could not help but wonder if her own Kevin felt the same way about her. She knew he loved her and all, but they were just teenagers. This Kevin was so mature and talked like a true adult. But, again, maybe it was his disease that had made him this way.

Steve came in the evening, as they had planned the day before. It was time for Anna to go home. She had mixed feelings about going. She wanted to go home; she wanted to see her own Kevin. She missed him a lot; she wanted to hug him and kiss him and tell him everything about this side. She decided to give it another try. He just had to believe her. And he should understand her plan. He would…or she just really hoped he would.

But at the same time, Anna wanted to stay here. She liked Steve. She was finally able to feel what it meant to have a father. And, if someone were to ask her, it was a great feeling. To have an adult in her life who cared, supported, and protected. Who was on her side no matter what. Anna realized that she had craved feeling this way her whole life…

But now it was really time to go. Anna said her goodbyes to Steve in the car. He hugged her tight and told her that he was already eager to see her again. Anna smiled at him and thanked him one more time.

Then Anna got out of the car and walked toward the coffee shop. Kevin went with her. Anna could see that he was shivering even though it wasn't very cold outside. She didn't know if that was because she was leaving him or because he was very weak from his illness. Anna decided not to ask.

The two young people stood there in front of the coffee shop, looking at one another. Each of them was searching for the right words.

"Thanks for coming again, Anna. You can't know how much it means for me and how much I appreciate it. All this craziness, as you call it, is a gift from Heaven for me. Or that's how I see it." Kevin's voice was soft.

"I will see you soon, Kevin." Anna felt like she was choking on her words.

"Are you sure about this whole plan?"

"Absolutely," Anna claimed, trying to sound more confident than she actually felt.

"You still don't know how you'll get back…after…I mean after I…" Anna saw that he couldn't say it out loud.

"You don't worry about it. I will figure something out, especially since I have Steve's help now. I won't be alone."

"Okay."

"I'll see you soon, Kevin."

Kevin didn't say anything else. Anna saw that he was trying to fight the tears gathering in his eyes. Then he opened the door to the coffee shop and held it wide open for her.

Anna hesitated for just for a brief moment, and then she went inside.

Thirty-One

The feeling was stronger this time: it was real exhaustion, like she hadn't slept or eaten for days. The moment she was back on her side, she felt the difference. She had never been gone for so long before, and now she needed to figure out what day it was and how long she had been gone from her own reality. Her phone was dead, and she didn't see Robin. There was a new barista behind the counter, but he was busy cleaning up so Anna decided to head straight home.

On her way home, Anna's mind was racing. *How do I tell Kevin? I will tell him. That's not even a question, but how do I tell him so that he believes me and agrees with my plan? How will I make him understand that I'm doing this for him? ...even if it's him on the other side, it's still him, Kevin, the one I love!*

As Anna approached her home, she wondered if there would be any food in the apartment. She was starving, and she felt very close to collapse if she didn't eat something in the next few minutes.

"Anna!" Kevin's voice startled her. It was loud and came from nowhere. Anna looked around and saw Kevin coming toward her. He must have been waiting for her by her apartment building.

For how long? How long have I been gone?

"Kevin! I'm so happy to see you!" Honestly, Anna felt stupid saying those words. It was like nothing had happened, like she hadn't been gone for days. But she was genuinely happy to see him, so she said the first words that came to mind.

A flood of words came from Kevin. "Where've you been? Anna! You've been gone for almost a whole month! I was losing my mind! The police were looking for you everywhere. Your mom's worried. Everyone's worried. Are you okay? What *happened?*"

Almost one month? No way. That's longer than I thought. Oh my goodness, I'm in trouble. I don't know if Kevin will listen to me now. But I need to try.

Anna started walking again, talking as she went. "Let's just go inside and talk. I'm starving, and I'm exhausted. I really just wanna go in and eat." Anna looked back at Kevin, but he wasn't following. He was just standing in the same spot and staring at her.

"Kevin? Are you coming?"

"Anna, are you for real? You disappear for a *freaking month*, and now all you're telling me is that you're hungry and tired. Is that *all?*"

"Oh, for goodness sake, Kevin! Do you really want us to talk here? Or should we go inside?!" Anna was becoming annoyed. Although Anna could understand Kevin's upset, her strong hunger and the desire to get into the apartment where they could speak privately were making it hard for her to empathize with him in the moment. They weren't on the same page.

Kevin didn't say anything but did follow her inside. Anna opened the door to the apartment and was relieved to see her mom not at home. She dropped her backpack on the floor, took her shoes off, and went straight to the kitchen.

"Are you hungry? Seems like we have some food here," Anna yelled back to Kevin, who was still standing in the living room.

"No, I'm not hungry." Anna heard the tension in Kevin's voice. She didn't like it. She knew that the upcoming conversation would not be easy, and she was dreading the undoubted argument. She hated it whenever they argued.

Nevertheless, Anna went on preparing food and making two cups of coffee. Kevin came into the kitchen in a few minutes and sat down. Anna put his cup in front of him.

"Sugar?"

"Anna! Where have you been?" Kevin was more than loud; he was practically yelling at her.

"Why are you yelling?"

"Because you can't disappear like that and then come back and pretend nothing happened and busy yourself with making us coffee. You clearly don't see the situation the way I see it."

"Maybe I don't. You're right. But I can explain."

"Go on. I'm listening."

Anna lost her appetite. Kevin's voice was so harsh, and she didn't like his tone of voice at all. She kept telling herself that he had every right to be mad. He had been worried about her. But she didn't know how to tell him everything with him in such a mood. Then she reminded herself that she didn't have a choice. She refused to lie to him.

"Kevin, remember I was telling you about the other side?"

"Anna, stop it. Please don't even go there. Not again. I thought we were done talking about any freaking mysterious other side... you, seeing yourself, your mom, and even me. Sounds very unconvincing to me. Just a very convenient excuse for being gone for who knows how long!"

"Kevin, please calm down. Hear me out. I'm not lying to you. I'll tell you everything as it is, I promise. You just have to listen to me, and you have to trust me."

"Where have you been for almost a month?" Kevin's tone was the same, not a bit softer.

"I just told you! I was on the other side! Believe it or not, it's your choice...but it does exist!

I didn't spend a whole month there, though. I was there only about two days, but time passes by differently over there. It's only moments there while it's hours over here. I don't know how different the time is exactly, but it's very different. I didn't want to disappear for so long."

"Oh my goodness...Do you really think I'll believe such nonsense? Just be brave enough to tell me the *truth*. Where have you been?"

"Kevin! I promise I'm telling you the absolute truth. Why can't you just take my word for it? Why don't you believe me? And I did all this for you!"

"What? For me? How is anything about this for me?"

"I told you about you on that side. Kevin is sick. He's *literally* dying. And Ann, or me on that side, broke up with him. He's so lonely. He needed me there, and he still needs me. You do."

Kevin's eyes got wider and wider as she was telling him about 'that Kevin.' His expression, though, clearly indicated that he didn't believe Anna. Maybe he even thought that she was insane.

But Anna wasn't! Everything was so clear in her head finally. Why was it so complicated to explain to others? Why couldn't she find the right words?

Kevin stared at Anna a moment more, then got up and went toward the door.

"Kevin! Are you leaving?" He didn't answer, but his actions spoke for him. He was putting his shoes on, getting ready to leave.

"Can I call you tomorrow? Kevin? Do you work tomorrow? Can we meet and talk again? Just say something! Don't ignore me!" Anna was boiling inside, she was so mad, frustrated, and upset.

"I don't know." That was all he said. Then he opened the door, walked out, closed it quietly, and left.

Anna was left standing alone in the middle of the living room. She felt lost and alone. She didn't know how to fix the situation. But Anna knew that she needed to hurry up and come up with a viable solution because she had only two days until it was time to go back.

Thirty-Two

The two days had passed, but Anna didn't find any solution. It's not like she didn't try. Oh boy, she did try her best, but nothing worked. She tried texting Kevin again and again. She attempted to call him repeatedly, but he didn't respond.

Anna even went to the pizzeria where Kevin worked, and she waited for him to get off, but Kevin was deliberately cruel to her. He left work through the back door, but Anna only found out hours later after she finally had the nerve to ask the manager for Kevin. Anna cried, but she was still determined to keep trying.

It was too late to go to Kevin's house that night, so Anna went there the next morning. She only missed him by minutes, according to Kevin's sister Katie. Anna didn't know if Katie was telling her the truth or if Kevin had asked Katie to tell Anna that he was at work.

Anna didn't give up even then. She went to the pizzeria once again, only to find out that Kevin had started delivering pizzas as of last week, so he would be out on deliveries most of the day. Of course, Anna knew that he would show up at some points, but she didn't get a chance to talk to him.

Every time Kevin came back into the pizzeria, he looked busy and cold, and he told Anna that she would have to wait. So she did. She waited, as long as she could. But the time was coming, and Anna knew that she had to go pretty soon. Anna almost cried in frustration.

What do I do now? I can't leave like this! I just can't! But I can't not go neither. I promised.

I don't know if I will get the chance again! Steve should bring Ann and her mom to the coffee shop today. If I don't show up, how will I know when they're going to be there again?

And I don't have weeks or months again to get there. Kevin probably doesn't have that much time left. Oh God, what do I do?

All of a sudden, though, Anna had an idea. *A letter! I will write him a letter!*

So, she took out a notebook and a pencil and started writing, praying that she had the right words.

Kevin, My Dearest Kevin,

You have no idea how hard all this is for me. I wish everything was easy and transparent in our relationship. I actually tried for the transparency, but it didn't work because you didn't believe me. To be honest, I don't blame you. I'm not sure I would believe my crazy story if I were you.

But the thing is, the other side exists, and I have been there enough times to stop questioning my sanity. I don't know why this started happening to me. It just did. I was thinking that this could be some genetic thing. I didn't have the chance to tell you, but I met my father on that side, He is technically that Ann's father, but it doesn't matter. He is a very good man. He is the steady parent that I have never really had in my life here.

Anyway, he told me that he saw me (the actual ME!) several times at the coffee shop. But he was never brave enough to approach me or to come over to this side. This all sounds and is so strange, but it gave me an idea that this could be some genetic thing. I hope that it's not a disease or anything. Maybe it's a super power? He-he. Like I said, I don't know.

Well, the thing is, that Kevin on the other side is not doing so great. He is sick. He is dying, Kevin…and it breaks my heart that that Ann (who is the love of his life) broke up with him! It's all so unfair…I would never do something cruel like that. I almost feel responsible for her cruelty; I wanna make it better for him. So, I am going to go back to that side. Today. In a few hours, actually. I have it all set up. I must go today. I don't know if I will have the chance again if I don't go today.

It breaks my heart that I am leaving you here like this, though. You and I didn't talk properly, and it hurts my heart. I want you to believe me, and I want you to wait for me. Know that I will come back when I can. I promise I will. I'm simply going there to spend time with Kevin during his final days (or hopefully months), and then I will come back.

The thing is, I don't know how much time will pass here. Remember that I mentioned the time difference between the two sides? So, it's definitely going to be longer here for you than it's going to be there for me…

Kevin, please forgive me for this. I hope you find enough strength and kindness within your heart to forgive me and to understand my actions. Knowing you, I wanna believe that you will. Please remember, I love you. I always did, and I always will.

Yours, Anna

Anna read through the letter one final time and then folded it in half. She simply wrote "for Kevin" on top of it and then went to the cash register. Once there, Anna asked to speak to the manager, praying in her heart for him to be available. She didn't trust giving the letter to anybody else, but she trusted the manager since he had been a friend of Kevin's dad.

Anna didn't know what she would do if the man was not available. At this point, Anna didn't have enough time left to go back to Kevin's house. But luck was on her side. The manager was available, and he promised to give the private letter to Kevin.

It was so hard to leave, though. Anna knew that her future depended on this person. If Kevin did not get her letter, he would have no idea where she was. And she had a feeling that she was going to be gone a long while this time. She didn't want to guess how long it would to be. She was simply too nervous for that.

But Anna felt that she didn't have any other choice. She handed the letter to the manager, feeling like she was handing her life and her fate into his hands. And then Anna left the pizzeria still wondering when she would see this place and her own Kevin again.

Thirty-Three

*A*nna was sitting at her corner table and anxiously waiting. She had come to the coffee shop fifteen minutes prior, but she was about ten minutes late for the agreed upon time. She'd had to stop at her apartment to leave a note for her mom. Writing that note wasn't as easy as Anna had thought it would be, but in the end, she managed to write a short note asking her mom not to worry about her and promising to come back in the future. She didn't want to disappear on her mom again without telling her anything, even if she wasn't the world's best mother. If anyone would have asked Anna, her mom still deserved to know.

But because everything had taken Anna so long, she was late in getting to the coffee shop, and with every passing minute, she was worrying more and more that she had missed Steve, Ann, and Maria. If they had come to get to-go drinks like they usually did, there was the distinct chance that she had missed them. And that was only if Steve had been able to convince Ann and her mom to come to the coffee shop in the first place. He had told Anna that he was going to try, but she was sure that it was easier to say than to do.

Please, God, just help me this one more time…I know I've done so many bad things in my life. I regret everything I've ever done wrong, like stealing and arguing with my mom and Kevin. But I really wanna make it better. I wanna help Kevin. I don't want him to be alone during his final days. I wanna do something good in my life! At least for once! Please make this happen, please…

As Anna was still saying her silent prayer, she saw the coffee shop door open and several people came in. Among them, she saw Steve and Maria. She didn't see Ann.

Is it going to work if she's not here? Oh it better work. I will have to try. It's not like I have a choice anyway.

Steve glanced at Anna, and she saw a slight nod from him, an almost imperceptible one, but she saw it. Anna smiled back and grabbed her backpack while she kept sitting at her table. She needed to keep this quiet. She was sure that it wasn't easy for Steve to arrange this meeting, and Ann was probably still too mad to talk to him.

A few minutes later with drinks in their hands, Steve and Maria headed toward the front door. Anna stood up and followed them. She was so tense and anxious.

Will it work without Ann being here? Will Steve remember to let Maria hold the door?

Anna observed how awkward it was for Steve not to open and hold the door for Maria. She saw the surprise in Maria's eyes while Anna mentally thanked Steve for following every step they had talked about. And then Steve was outside and Maria was still holding the door.

It's time. Here I come. Now!

Anna grabbed the door while Maria was still touching it and stepped closer. Then she looked up and their eyes met. The next moment felt like an eternity. Anna saw how shocked Maria looked when she saw Anna's face. Maria looked like she wanted to say something, but she hesitated just for a second, and that was enough time for Anna to blurt out her "excuse me" and start walking out from the coffee shop. Her heart was racing and she felt a rush of adrenaline going through her body.

Anna went around the corner, and then she stopped. She just stood there behind the coffee shop, with her back against the cold wall of the building, taking deep breaths in and out and willing herself to calm down.

It's okay. You did it. It worked. It worked! She's not going to follow you. Steve will distract her. It'll be fine. Now go directly to Steve's house and meet him there, just like you planned.

Self-talk was a powerful thing. Anna felt a lot better. She started walking away from the coffee shop, but then something inside of her made her glance back. For a moment, she thought that it was her imagination, but then she looked closer and saw him. Kevin was there. He was at the coffee shop! He came. He had followed her!

Anna ran back to look at Kevin through the window. There he was, looking lost and even confused. He was clutching a piece of paper in his hand...her letter...looking around like he was searching for something...or for someone. Anna's heart ached for him. He was so close, yet so far away...on the other side.

Anna desperately wanted to go back, to talk to him, to explain everything now, when he was ready to talk to her. But how could she? She didn't think it was possible without this side's Ann, Maria, or Kevin being here.

Should I try? Oh God, I don't know. What should I do? I really wanted for this to happen. I even prayed for this to happen, and now when I made it to the other side, what do I want now?

I need to make up my mind. I need to be here for Kevin. Yes, I promised him. But my Kevin…I hope he'll understand. I hope my letter is enough…

Anna stood there with tears in her eyes, feeling like she was making the hardest decision ever. Unable to move, unable to cry out loud, she was silently choking on her own tears.

Then she saw Kevin moving toward the front door. He was leaving. Anna rushed toward the door, hoping for one crazy second that they could meet. But they didn't. Anna saw Kevin leaving the coffee shop, but he didn't appear in front of her like she hoped he would. He was gone. And she was on the other side. Again.

Thirty-Four

Anna slowly walked toward Steve's house. She didn't know why she didn't try to walk faster, to finally see him, to talk about the past few days, to plan further. Instead, she kept walking slowly, feeling very sad deep inside.

Anna wasn't exactly sure why she was feeling the way she did, but she felt like she had just lost something very important. She felt like something terrible had happened. Or maybe something terrible was about to happen? Anna didn't know.

What Anna did recognize was her instinctive feeling of loss, like it was the biggest one in her life. Anna just hoped that she didn't lose the love of her life, her Kevin. Anna hoped that her plan wasn't a mistake that would cost her too much—more than she could bear.

Despite her dejected feelings, Anna started looking around, paying attention to her surroundings, noticing slight differences between both sides. It was so interesting to observe and pay attention to the little things, the differences.

Like the old house on the other side of the street—its framing around the windows were supposed to be red, but they were blue here. And there were lacy curtains upstairs, something Anna had never seen on her side. They were little things, unimportant differences really, but that was part of someone's life.

Some differences were more important than the color around the windows, though. Kevin. Here he was dying from leukemia while her Kevin was strong and healthy. Herself. She was crazy in love with Kevin, but Ann wasn't anymore…

Anna slowly approached Steve's house. There she saw his car, neatly parked in the driveway. Next to the car, Anna noticed a cat. It was gray colored with blue eyes and small ears. Its presence was strange, though, because she didn't know Steve had a cat.

Maybe it's not his…maybe the cat is just wandering around.

Anna was within a few feet of the house, but she didn't attempt to go in. She just stood there, unable to move. She still felt very sad. It was like she was saying goodbye to her life on the other side. She couldn't understand why she felt this way, but she did, and it was scaring her.

I will find a way to get back home once this is over. Right? I'll figure something out. There must be a way to get back, even after Kevin is no longer here. It's not like I'll be gone from my side for good. I will get back. I will see my mom again, and of course, I'll see Kevin again. He will be waiting for me. He got my letter; he followed me; he loves me. I will find a way to get back to him. I will.

Then why did Anna feel so sad and apprehensive?

Part 2

Thirty-Five

"Anna! Finally! Come on in. Why'd it take you so long to come here? Is everything okay?" Steve looked at her like he was searching for something.

"Hi, Steve. Yes, I'm fine. Everything's okay. Are you alone?"

"Of course, I'm alone. You look a little...sad?"

"No, no, everything is great, really. I was just stressed about the whole thing and then when mom...Maria looked at me like that at the coffee shop, my heart sank."

"Oh, that! Yeah, she was shaken herself. She kept asking if I saw the girl at the coffee shop who looked so much like our Ann. I had to pretend that I had no idea what she was talking about, but it was harder to distract her than I thought it would be.

She kept talking about you. Then she texted Ann, and then she called her because she wasn't answering. For half a second, she thought you were Ann.

She even had a whole story in a matter of seconds about Ann missing school and pretending to be someone else. She connected Ann's stealing to all this. Anyway, I think I was finally able to convince her that she saw someone who just looked like Ann."

"Thank you, Steve. Thank you for making this possible. I'm sure it wasn't easy for you to organize all this being divorced from Maria and all."

"And I wasn't able to properly organize everything anyway. Ann is still refusing to talk to me. She's still too mad about the whole divorce thing. She makes it so much harder, especially for Maria…I didn't know if it's going to work without Ann, but I had to try."

"Yeah, when I saw it was just you and Maria, I freaked out for a second. I haven't done this enough to completely understand how everything works—but it worked and that's the most important thing."

"Well, come on in. Don't just stand here. Have a seat while I fix some food for us. Tell me everything. How's your mom? Did you talk to her?

And how's your Kevin? Were you able to explain everything to him? Did he accept your decision?"

That was the moment when Anna couldn't pretend any longer that she was 'fine' and everything was 'great.' She started sobbing.

Steve took one look at her, and then he came closer and held her in his strong arms while she cried it out. Anna bawled until she ran out of tears, until she was ready to talk again.

She hoarsely stated, "I'm so scared, Steve."

"I know you are. It's not too late, though. We can probably get you back to the other side tonight. And you can just live your life and pretend like all this never happened. It's your right to do so!"

"But how could I do that?!"

"Just as I did…it was easier that way."

"No! I made my decision. I wanna do this. I just…I just…I'm so scared to lose Kevin. I love him too much. Is that stupid?"

"No! Of course, it's not stupid. What you have and feel is beautiful. Not everyone is lucky enough to experience love the way you and Kevin have."

"But we're so young. Most people would probably say it's not serious. They think that we're just foolish kids—that true love will come later in life."

"Anna, they don't know that. And since when do you care what others say or think? It's their problem what they think. This is your life!

I'm telling you that I'm very proud of you for being able to love the way you do. What you're doing for Kevin on this side is simply incredible, and it shows how much you love Kevin overall. You care enough to do this. This is just…simply amazing!"

"But I am scared…so scared that I'm making a mistake. I'm scared to lose my Kevin. What if he won't wait for me? What if I'm never able to get back to the other side again?

What if this Kevin is the only way to get back? And after… after he is…you know…what if that was my last time talking to my Kevin? Oh, Steve, I don't think I'd be able to handle that!"

"Anna, oh Anna…you have a hard decision to make here. And it has to be completely yours. Don't think about others. Just think about how you feel about this."

"Well…," Anna paused for a long moment, "…like I said, the decision has been made. Steve, I just wanted to talk to you about my feelings. Thank you for listening and supporting me in this. Thank you for making this possible."

Steve didn't say anything. He simply hugged her one more time and then they just sat there quietly, each still thinking about what had been said.

"Steve?" Anna was the first one to talk again.

"Yes?" Steve looked almost surprised, like he had forgotten that Anna was sitting next to him.

"Can I call Kevin? I wanna tell him that I'm here and will be coming to see him shortly."

"Of course. Here's my phone. And we need to go to the store tomorrow to get you one as well. You'll need a phone that works here."

Anna didn't say anything, she just nodded and then she went into Steve's office to call Kevin so that they could talk privately.

While Anna was gone, Steve busied himself in the kitchen, mixing salad and planning to open a frozen pizza and throw it in the oven once the over preheated.

Anna came back a few minutes later, the color drained from her face.

"He's at the hospital. I just talked to his mom."

"Kevin's at the hospital? Is he all right?" Steve stopped chopping cucumbers.

"I don't know exactly, but his mom started crying when she heard me talking and just said that Kevin's very sick, has been at the hospital since last night, and is asking for me when he's awake."

"Did you ask her which hospital and if you can go see him?" Steve was trying to stay calm and think logically.

"No, I didn't!" Anna blurted, in disbelief at her own stupidity.

"Then go call his mom again."

"Okay."

Steve waited for Anna in the kitchen. He thought about life and how it could be so unfair. Kids should not go through something like that. Kids should not be dying from cancer. Kids shouldn't know how it is to lose love due to death at such a young age. Nobody should, but especially not kids. Life just wasn't fair sometimes…

"Steve? Are you okay?" Anna's voice brought him back to reality.

"Ah? Yes, yes. What did she say?"

"She said that it's too late to go see him today, but I can go first thing in the morning. Visiting hours start at eight o'clock. And I wrote down how to find him."

"Good. Then we're going to go there first thing in the morning. Now let's have something to eat. I bet you're starving."

Anna was exhausted. She probably was starving as well, but she was too tired to think. She simply obeyed and sat down. Steve put a plate in front of her and she started eating.

They both ate their dinner in silence. And it felt okay, to sit next to Steve and just be completely quiet.

Thirty-Six

The next day Anna was ready to go see Kevin just a little after sunrise. But it was too early, so she had to wait. Anna didn't like waiting, and she felt anxious.

How sick is he? What will we talk about? Will I manage not to cry in front of him? With these thoughts, Anna went into Steve's office, the only place she felt comfortable going without him being around. There, she found shelves full of different books.

It was like his own little library.

Wow! I didn't know someone could have so many books at home. I'll have to ask him how many of these he's read. There's no way one person could have read so many books.

Anna ran her right index finger over the spines, scanning some of the names. Some books were familiar to her; some looked interesting while others looked boring. Suddenly, Anna saw one that she had already read, and she felt almost proud. Then she picked a book from amongst the shelves and decided to read while waiting for Steve to wake up and take her to the hospital.

Reading made waiting easier, and Anna was grateful. After Steve came downstairs and they had breakfast together, they were finally ready to go see Kevin.

"Okay, let's do this! Which hospital is he at?" Steve looked enthusiastic, and Anna wonder if he really felt that cheerful or if he was just trying to portray optimism for her sake.

"Let me look at that paper again. Here, I wrote everything down," said Anna and then gave him the yellow sticky note.

"Shoot!" Steve didn't look so optimistic all of a sudden.

"What's the matter? Is it that far away?" Anna wasn't familiar with the hospitals as she had never stayed or gone to one. If she was sick, Tylenol was her doctor.

"No, it's not. But that's the hospital where Maria works."

"No way! I didn't know she worked at the hospital! Is she one of the nurses or doctors there?"

"No. She's that hospital's CEO."

"CEO?" Anna wasn't sure she knew what that meant.

"Yes. She's basically the main administrator or boss there...the head of the hospital."

"Well, that's better than a nurse. I guess, I have less chance of running into her while visiting Kevin in his room, right?" Now Anna was trying to be optimistic for both Steve and herself.

"That's right. But everyone knows Maria there, and I'm sure many people know Ann as she comes there frequently."

"Shoot! What should I do then?" Anna was ready for Steve to tell her that she wouldn't be able to go see Kevin until he was discharged home. But he surprised her again.

"You'll have to be careful. That's all. Now let's go. It's almost eight."

Thirty-Seven

Talking with Kevin felt good. Anna had missed him a lot, and now she was finally with him, in his hospital room sitting in the chair next to his bed. Kevin was smiling at her, his eyes bright.

"I'm so glad everything worked out okay! I bet Maria was confused when she saw you. You and Ann look so alike, yet so different...especially with your short hair."

"Did you see Maria at the hospital? I'm nervous about running into her."

"Oh no, I don't think you should worry about that. She's the CEO here. I don't think she's gonna be walking around checking on patients."

"Steve made it sound like many people know Ann at this hospital since she comes here all the time. I was thinking about the possibility of running into somebody who knows Ann. Do you think I should pretend that I am her, or should I pretend I have no idea what they're talking about and that my name's Felicia?"

"Felicia? Why Felicia?" Kevin laughed.

"I don't know! That's just the first name that came to mind. Kevin! Stop laughing! I'm serious." Anna was only half serious, though, and she enjoyed seeing him laugh.

"Honestly, I don't know. I think if it happens, you'll know what to do. But don't worry too much. I hope, I'll get to go home soon. I feel much better today than I did yesterday."

"Well, that's good!"

"Anna?" Kevin was suddenly serious.

"Yes?"

"What'll you do if you actually run into Ann herself? ...here at the hospital or somewhere else?"

Anna didn't know what to say. She thought about it, but she couldn't decide what she would do if it ever happened.

"Honestly, Kevin, I don't know."

"I think you should give it some thought and decide what you'd do because it could happen, you know."

Anna was quiet. He was right. She had some thinking to do.

Thirty-Eigth

Visiting hours went by quickly, and then it was time for Anna to go home. Well, she didn't really have a home on this side, but going to Steve's house felt right. He'd given her keys to the house, and he had given her money for lunch. Moreover, he had told her that he would take her to the store later that day to get her a phone because she should be able to get a hold of him if needed. Anna wasn't sure how to react. She definitely wasn't used to being treated like that. But she agreed. A new and working phone did sound good.

So, Anna said goodbye to Kevin and promised to text or call him later that day once she had a phone. She also promised to visit again first thing the next morning, but Kevin was absolutely sure that he would get discharged later in the day since he was feeling a lot better.

"Okay, then I'll come over to your place in the morning if that's all right."

"Sure! I'll be counting the hours until I see you again." Kevin smiled at her, and Anna felt strong satisfaction at making him happy. At that moment, she knew that she *had* made the right decision. He needed her now. And it felt good to be there for him. That was the least she could do given the situation.

Once Anna stepped outside, the sunshine was so strong in her eyes that she couldn't keep them open. It took her a minute to adjust, and then she started walking.

It was a gorgeous day for a walk, but somehow Anna felt sad again—sad about leaving her Kevin behind; sad about Kevin being sick in this reality; sad about him getting sicker and weaker; sad about not knowing if her mom was okay.

But then Anna remembered how Kevin had laughed, and how he looked at her every time she was around…yes, it was all worth it. His every smile was so dear to her! And she would do everything in her power to make him smile many more times before…before…Anna couldn't even finish that phrase in her head. She knew that *it* was going to happen, but she didn't want to think about that just yet.

It was a very long walk to Steve's house, but Anna didn't want to take the bus. She wasn't in a hurry anyway. Steve was at work, and she didn't know what to do with herself until the evening.

So, Anna just meandered, stopping here and there. She stopped at a little café to get a late lunch. After standing in the line for ten minutes, though, she decided that she wasn't that hungry, so she left.

Then she stopped by the art museum to look at big advertising boards all around it. Everything there looked fascinating. Anna had a strong desire to go in. She decided to go inside just to check the ticket price. To her surprise, youth tickets weren't expensive. Just moments later, with a big smile on her face, Anna was walking around looking at art exhibits and admiring most of them.

Time flew by at the museum. When Anna checked the time, she realized that she probably should get going if she wanted to meet Steve when he came home from work. And she felt hungry! But she definitely did not regret spending her lunch money for the ticket. It had been worth every penny. Anna couldn't wait to tell Steve and Kevin all about everything she had seen and learned today.

Anna wished that she already had a phone. She would have taken some pictures to show to Kevin.

Thirty-Nine

ey, Kevin, how r u doing? This is my number. We just got home. I cant believe I have an iPhone! Honestly Steve didnt have 2 buy me an expensive phone. Im nervous 2 drop it or something. Im not used 2 pricey things. Now, did u get discharged? Btw I'll tell u about my adventure! Went 2 art museum on way home. it was amazing! Have u been? Anna. PS. I know u know its me. Xo.

Anna pressed the send button and waited for Kevin's reply, but minutes ticked away, and he didn't respond.

R u ok? Hope u r just sleeping. Text me when u can. Anna sent him the next text.

Hey, Ann. Yeah, Im fine.

Anna wasn't sure what to think of the short reply.

Kevin what's going on?

Its nothing. nothing I wasnt expecting.

Kevin! What is it? Anna anxiously held her new iPhone like her life depended on it.

I didnt get discharged. My blood works terrible. My white counts 2 low. I just wanna go home. I dont care anymore. Im going to die anyway!!! Whats the point of keeping me here! I just have 2 get my mom to agree n then they might let me go home. on Hospice.

No, no, no. This cannot happen so soon, oh, Kevin no…what do I say? How do I make him feel better? Oh God… Anna's thoughts were chaotic. She couldn't think what to text back.

Anna even didn't know what "low white count" meant, but she was sure that it was bad. She knew that Kevin's mood was nothing like she had encountered before. He must be depressed, mad, frustrated. She didn't know, but she needed to find a way to make him feel better…if that was even possible.

Oh Lord Kevin, I'm sorry 2 hear. Can I visit u in the morning? Anna felt stupid sending him that reply, but she couldn't come up with anything else.

Yes. Ill b here…not going anywhere. C u then. Gnight.

Anna wanted to talk more. She wish she'd just called him instead. She wanted to tell Kevin about her day, and she wanted to hear him talk. Or she wanted to just text with him all night long while talking about simple things. But Kevin obviously didn't feel the same.

Good night. Anna sent her response, and then she turned her brand new iPhone off. She wasn't even excited about it any longer.

Forty

Anna slept restlessly that night. She kept having nightmares that woke her up. At one point, she sat up in bed and got her phone to check if there was anything from Kevin. She was worried that he would get much sicker during the night. There was nothing from him.

Anna prayed silently for the morning to come sooner and for a Kevin to get better, and then she went back to sleep. However, it wasn't until dawn when she finally fell asleep deeply enough to get some rest.

When she woke up, there was still nothing from Kevin, no missed calls, no texts. Anna was too nervous to call or text, so she just waited for Steve to get ready. Shortly thereafter, they left the house without grabbing any breakfast because neither of them felt like eating.

Steve convinced Anna to get an apple to go. She grabbed two—the biggest one for Kevin. And then Steve took her to the hospital on his way to work.

When Anna arrived at the hospital, she felt on the verge of tears. She told herself to calm down several times while she was heading to the third floor and then to room eleven, Kevin's room.

There, she stood for a moment, barely giving any attention to the big sign on his door. "Neutropenic Precautions" read the sign. Anna didn't know what it meant. She opened the door and saw Kevin laying in the bed, eyes open.

"Good morning!" said Anna as cheerfully as she could.

"Hey, there. Nice to see you." Kevin gave her a weak smile.

"How've you been? Got some rest last night?" Anna felt like she was asking the wrong questions.

"Yeah." And then there was an awkward silence.

"Well, that's good. Did you eat anything yet?" It was the wrong question again.

"No. Not hungry." Kevin wasn't looking at her.

"Want an apple?" Anna held her hand out, showing Kevin the apple she had chosen for him.

"Sure. Thanks. How was your day yesterday?" Kevin took a bite from the apple and was looking at her now.

It was a good sign.

Anna sat on the bed next to Kevin and started eating her apple as well. She wasn't hungry, but it was easier to talk this way. So, she told Kevin about her visit to the art museum. She didn't feel as enthusiastic as she had the day before, but she tried to look happy.

While Anna was still talking and both were still crunching on their apples, there was a knock on the door. The door opened, and Anna saw a nurse coming in with a little tray of medicine.

"Hey there. How are you feeling, Kevin? I'm Monica, your day-shift nurse." Monica smiled, but then the smile looked weird, almost painful.

"Who gave you that apple?" Monica didn't look so friendly anymore. Her voice was loud, her tone stern.

Anna wasn't sure what was happening.

"I did," she quietly said.

"Didn't you see the sign on the door?!" Monica's voice rose. She was almost yelling at this point.

"What sign?" For some reason Anna felt like she was in trouble.

"The Neutropenic Precautions sign!" Monica was yelling now.

"Um…I did, but I didn't know what it meant." Anna felt scared.

"That's why you have to read it! I'm sure you know how to read! Kevin can't have any fresh fruits or flowers or pets or anything! He can die! Do you understand? That's what that sign means, and you would have known that if you would have taken a minute to read it! It's there for a reason!"

Anna felt her eyes filling up with tears. She was so scared—scared of Monica yelling at her; scared of being in trouble again; scared that the nurses would not allow her to visit again. And most of all, Anna was scared that she had unwittingly harmed Kevin. He could die because of her.

Before Anna had a chance to say anything, she saw another nurse approaching the room. This one looked older than Monica and that fact terrified Anna even more.

"What in the world is going on here, Monica? What are you yelling about?" the older nurse asked.

"Theresa, sorry I was so loud. I got very upset because Kevin's visitor didn't look at the precaution sign and gave him the apple to eat. His white count is dangerously low."

Theresa looked at a Kevin; then she looked at Anna, assessing the situation. Anna was hoping with all her heart that Theresa would say something, like it wasn't a big deal and Anna just shouldn't do it again. Instead, what she said sent Anna into even bigger shock.

"Ann? Does your mom know you're here? I'll go call her. Monica, come with me."

Both nurses left the room. Kevin was silently looking at Anna. Anna felt like her heart couldn't race any faster than it was already.

"Kevin, I'm so very sorry! I should have read that sign! I can't believe how stupid I am!" Anna was crying at this point. She couldn't control her emotions any longer.

"Anna, don't be sorry. It's not your fault. I knew about the neutropenic precautions, but I just don't care any longer. If I want an apple, I'll eat the freaking apple. I'm ready. Now that you're here with me, I'm ready."

"Ready for what?!" There was a terror in Anna's voice.

"I'm ready to die. I can't go on much longer like this. This is not the life I would choose for myself." Kevin was serious and calm.

"Kevin! Don't say that!"

"Let's talk about it later. Theresa's a manager for this unit. She came yesterday during morning rounds. I'm sure she's calling Maria now, Ann's mom. I think you should leave before I get you into an even bigger mess."

Anna didn't know what to say or do. She wanted to say so much more to Kevin, but she definitely wasn't ready to meet Maria face to face.

Anna hesitated just for a second, then she leaned toward Kevin and kissed him on his pale cheek.

"Call me or text me when you can. Sorry about all this again."

Anna was walking toward the door when she heard a very quiet, "I love you." It was so quiet that she wasn't sure if she heard it or if she had imagined it.

She didn't turn around to check.

Forty-One

I am not ready for Kevin to go. Not yet. I wasn't expecting every-thing to happen so fast. It's just not fair! I thought that I'd have months with him or at least several weeks. But he acts like he wants to die today! Not that he is just ready for that, but he really wants to die! What an idiot!

I'm so mad at that boy right now. Why didn't Kevin just tell me he couldn't have that stupid apple?!

Why didn't I read that bloody sign on the stupid door? And what's going to happen now when that nurse calls Ann's mom? Oh God, I don't know anything anymore.

I feel like I am in so much trouble. I didn't want any of this to happen. I just wanted to come to this side to help Kevin, be there for him. He's seemed so lonely every time I've seen him, and now that idiot acts like he can't wait to die, even though I'm here. What a mess…

Anna kept walking, completely lost in her thoughts. She kept blaming herself for not reading the sign, and she kept blaming Kevin for eating her apple. Finally, she couldn't think about any of it anymore.

It happened. Everything happened already. I can't change any-thing now. I just have to wait and see what's going to happen next.

Anna kept walking without any particular destination in mind. She didn't want to go to Steve's house, but she didn't have anywhere else to go.

Before she realized where her feet were taking her, Anna was standing in front of the coffee shop—the place where the crazy story had begun. If it wasn't for the coffee shop, she believed that she would be home right now, enjoying her summer break, seeing Kevin on his days off, counting down the days until her sixteenth birthday. Anna decided to go in.

Once inside, Anna ordered a drink and a small pastry, and then she went to take her usual table at the corner. But, to her surprise, the table was already taken. She saw an old man sitting there while sipping on his coffee and reading the newspaper. That had never happened on her side. The table was hers. She never saw anyone sitting there, ever.

I guess I better get used to this. How weird, though…

Anna took another table and sat down. She nibbled on her morning bun and sipped her cappuccino. Both tasted great, but she felt full before she was even halfway done. Her mind was elsewhere.

While still lost in her thoughts, Anna felt her phone vibrating in her pocket. She took it out and saw a text message from Kevin.

Im going home!

Another text came just seconds later.

I convinced mom 2 sit down n talk. She finally listened n heard me. Im going home soon!

Before Anna had a chance to process what that meant, she got a third text.

Any chance u can visit me @ home later?

Of course. what time? Anna texted him back.

Ill let u know 4 sure n a little. The nurse is working on all the discharge stuff. I feel bad for Monica. Im probably her worst pt today. Oh well…Im going home! Thats all I care about.

Anna's thoughts swirled in turmoil. *I can see that…That's really all he cares about. Never mind eating that damn apple that could have killed him. Never mind me being all scared and stressed out. He is going home! To die probably. Oh Kevin. Why do I love you and care so much about you?!*

She texted Kevin back. *Monica will b fine. See you later. Btw, did Maria come after I left?*

She did.

And? Anna prompted.

And what?

Kevin, u know what I mean! Just tell me what happened!

Kevin answered. *I told her that Ann stopped by this morning. but just for a few minutes. Maria was surprised, I think. But I hope she'll leave it @ that n won't ask Ann anything.*

I dont think so. I have a weird feeling that she will n this story's not done.

Anny, don't worry, everything will be fine.

U r right, Kevin. That's easy to say…but I feel like nothing will b fine!

Anna's soul was screaming inside when another text came.

Ok. I gotta go, Anna. the nurses here. Talk 2 u later.

Talk 2 u later, Kevin.

Forty-Two

*L*ater that day, when it was almost evening, Anna went to see Kevin at his home. By that time, she felt calmer, and she had almost half convinced herself that maybe he is right and everything would be fine.

Talking to Steve had definitely helped. Having a conversation with the adult had worked like magic for Anna, maybe because she always lacked that steady influence in her own life on the other side.

Anna greeted Elizabeth who was happy to see her, just like Kevin's mom on the side would always do. Elizabeth was so very nice, and she immediately welcomed Anna into the house after opening the front door.

"Come on in, dear. Kevin's in his room. He'll be happy you're here." Although Elizabeth's words held their typical warmth, Anna detected sadness in her voice. Anna guessed that the conversation the woman had with her son earlier that day must not have been easy for her. How could it have been anything but difficult.

Many thoughts floated through Anna's brain. *Does it mean she has given up on him, if she has let him come home while being so sick? How do you give up on your own child?! Or does she love him enough to respect what he wants, even if it means a sooner death? I can't possibly know how hard all this is for her, poor woman. No mother should go through this.*

"Thank you, I'm happy to be here for him," said Anna.

"I'm glad you came back into his life, Ann. Kevin really needs you, especially now. I think he needs you more than he needs me. I can't tell you enough how grateful I am to you for coming back."

"Elizabeth…" Anna paused. She felt she needed to tell her. Anna didn't want to lie to her, but she didn't know how to explain, what to say.

Where do I even start?! And, honestly, her son's dying…does the rest even really matter at this point?

"…you're welcome. Sorry for being gone for so long," said Anna instead, and then she went to see Kevin in his room.

Anna saw that Kevin was asleep in his bed. He looked different than he had that morning. It was difficult to place just what was different, but something inexplicable had really changed since she saw him at the hospital.

Anna didn't want to wake Kevin up. She sat down on the chair by the table where Kevin probably used to sit a lot before he got sick, doing his homework and reading.

There she saw a photo album with real printed pictures inside. She was surprised as she thought that no one had printed pictures anymore. It seemed like owning a fancy smartphone was enough for most people nowadays. Anna started flipping through the album pages.

There, she saw many pictures of Kevin and Ann, doing different activities together. Anna noticed that they had gone many places together, which was different from what she'd experienced on her life on the other side.

Anna and her Kevin had never had enough money to go to the water parks, museums, and fancy cafes. But it didn't really matter. What did matter was the fact that they had spent a lot of time together, loving each other. That seemed to be the same on both sides...until Ann broke up with Kevin. Anna wondered why Ann had broken up with Kevin. She could never imagine doing the same thing.

Anna finished flipping through the pictures and looked over at Kevin again. He was still sleeping. She finally realized what was different from that morning. His face was relaxed; his whole body was relaxed. He looked peaceful.

Only then did Anna notice that there was a bag hanging on a pole. It was attached to his bed. The bag had a small tube. Anna's eyes followed the path of the tubing down and saw that it was connected to Kevin's chest. Anna knew that it was his "chest port" because he had already told her that before. She didn't really know what that was, but Kevin had explained that it was like a "super intravenous line" so that he could get his cancer medicine through it.

Anna came closer to look at the bag. She saw that Kelvin's medicine was slowly dripping through the tube. The label on the bag simply read "Morphine."

Anna stared down at Kevin.

Morphine?! Even I know that's not a medicine to treat cancer. It's a pain killer. Kevin never told me he's in pain!

Oh God, is he suffering really bad? And he didn't even tell me anything. I'm so stupid...Of course he's suffering.

No wonder Kevin has wanted to go home and be done with everything. Who wants to lay in the hospital and suffer through pain when you know you're going to die soon anyway? That's not the way to spend your last days. No one deserves to die at the hospital surrounded by unfamiliar people, away from home and away from things that bring comfort!

If you ask me, everyone deserves to die at home when it comes to that. If the treatment fails and you know you're gonna die, it's time to go home—to be comfortable, to be peaceful.

Good for you, Kevin, on insisting on this! I'm so proud of you. I'm not mad at you no more. I just didn't understand anything but now I do. I will tell him exactly that when he wakes up.

Still lost in her thoughts, trying to sort through her emotions, Anna was startled when the bedroom door opened, and she saw Elizabeth. There was confusion on Elizabeth's face.

"Ann? You're still here?!" asked Elizabeth, looking at Anna and then at her sleeping son.

Then the door opened wider and Anna saw Ann. They were finally standing face to face...staring at each other.

Forty-Three

"*W*ho *are* you?!" Ann was the first one to speak. Her voice sounded demanding.

"I'm Anna," said Anna simply, like the answer was obvious.

Anna had pondered the possibility of this moment so many times, and she'd played different scenarios in her head and now, when it actually happened, she wasn't even nervous. She was looking at a different version of herself. Nevertheless, her brain still wondered.

Is it like looking in the mirror? Close enough. She is just like me, just...fancy.

Ann was still staring at Anna, dumbfounded.

"You look just like me..."

"I know." Anna remained calm.

"What else do you know that I don't? Can you freaking tell me what is going on here? My mom told me that I visited Kevin in the hospital this morning and caused trouble there. But I can tell you for sure that I didn't. That was you?" Ann spoke anxiously.

"Yeah, it was me."

"Well, who *are* you?! How..." continued Ann in a challenging manner.

"Ann, I'll tell you everything, I promise. But can we go for a walk? I don't wanna wake Kevin up. I think he's already had a rough enough day without this."

Anna hoped Ann would listen to her. She didn't want to talk in here, not in front on Elizabeth, not with the risk of waking up Kevin, and causing even more chaos.

Ann stared at Anna without saying anything. So, Anna took it upon herself. She grabbed Ann's hand and walked her out from Kevin's room and then pulled the other girl outside even as she was throwing a quick "I'm sorry" to Elizabeth on the way out.

It was easier to talk to Ann than Anna had expected. Ann listened carefully without interrupting and only asked questions after Anna was done with the story. Anna told Ann everything, starting with her own life on the other side and seeing Ann and Maria at the coffee shop for the first time and finishing with the story about Kevin eating the apple at the hospital that morning.

"Wow. I don't know what to say. Wow…," Ann stated, obviously shocked.

"Yeah…"

"Honestly, I would never have believed such a crazy story. It sounds like a whole bunch of nonsense. But you're here with me. I'm looking at you, talking to you, touching you. I can't really deny that this is real, can I?"

"No, Ann, you can't. It's real."

"And you said that my dad had already seen you at the coffee shop before? Have he been to your side?"

"He saw me. But no, he never went to my side," Anna answered.

"You know, it's sad...I was so mean to dad lately. And all because I was so mad at him for divorcing mom. I know it was her wanting the divorce, but I still blamed him.

If it wasn't for his crazy stories, mom would never have divorced him. We were a perfect family. I would like to think we were...I know we were happy! But now you're here, proving that he was telling the truth. Oh, I feel so guilty..."

"It's okay, Ann. Really, it is. He loves you, and he'll talk to you whenever you're ready. Just don't waste any more time being mad at him and blaming him. Honestly, you don't know how lucky you are having Steve in your life."

"You're right. I *will* call him today. I wanna talk to him. Well, I did all this time, but I was too mad, too stubborn, and didn't even want to hear him explain anything."

"Good. What about Kevin, though, Ann?" Anna asked her question carefully. She was almost scared to hear Ann's answer.

"I don't know, Anna. It's difficult."

"He loves you."

"I know he does."

"Do you? Do you really love him, Ann?"

There was a long, awkward pause.

"No. I don't think I do. I mean I do care for him, but... Oh, I'm such a horrible person..." Ann had tears in her eyes.

"It's okay, Ann. It's okay. Don't cry. That's why I'm here now. I'll take care of him. I'll not replace you for him, but I will do my best so he's not lonely in his final days."

"Thank you, Anna. Thank you so much for this."

And then the two girls just walked silently, both lost in their own troublesome thoughts—about the other side, about Steve, about the divorce, about Kevin laying in his bed with the Morphine infusing into his chest port...

Forty-Four

After the two girls finally parted and Anna went back to Kevin's house, it was already dark outside. The time she spent with Ann had gone by really fast as they had a lot to talk about and because talking to Ann was surprisingly super easy, like they had known each other all their lives. They agreed to get together again the next day, after which point Anna had gone back to see Kevin, and Ann decided to go see her father.

Anna was very nervous about having to explain everything to Elizabeth, but when she stood in front of the front door, hesitating about knocking, Elizabeth opened the door wide with a smile on her face.

"Come on in, dear. I was worrying about you. It's getting late. Don't stand there! Come on in! Kevin told me everything, so there's no need for you to worry about me. Okay?"

Wow, that was easier than I expected.

"You're not mad at me for not telling you the truth when I first came here?" Anna was surprised.

"Of course, I'm not mad. Let's be real… What are the chances that I would have believed your story? But seeing you and Ann together today didn't leave me any other choice," Elizabeth claimed, still smiling.

Anna finally stepped inside, took her shoes off, and went in to see Kevin. She knocked on his door and waited a second. There was no response, so she carefully opened the door and poked her head inside.

"Anna? Come in." Kevin's voice was very quiet.

"Hey, it's nice to see you home. How're you feeling?"

"I feel fine, but it's hard to keep my eyes open with this thing infusing constantly," Kevin stated while gesturing to his Morphine bag. "I can finally relax, though, and not be in pain all the time."

"You didn't tell me you were in pain. I'm so sorry. I had no idea. I feel so stupid because it's not rocket science, considering that you have cancer."

The moment Anna offered the words aloud, she felt very awkward. Talking about cancer was not her comfort zone. She thought if that she talked about the cancer, she was admitting it was real—she was accepting it.

Kevin must have sensed her discomfort. He tried to rescue her right away by changing the topic.

"How was it talking to Ann? Was she shocked? Tell me... everything."

"She was shocked, but talking to her was surprisingly easy. It was weird. I didn't expect to, but I enjoyed her company. We're even going to meet again tomorrow."

"Wow. That's nice. So, did she ask about me?" Anna noticed that Kevin's eyes were bright when he talked about Ann.

Did she? I don't think so. She said it all pretty loud and clear when she admitted that she doesn't love him. But I can't tell him that, can I? It would be too cruel. Anna felt terrible.

"Yeah, she wanted to know how you're doing and stuff." Anna felt uncomfortable uttering the blatant lie. She wanted to change the subject again, but couldn't think what else to talk about.

"So what did you tell her? What else did she say? What's she doing on her summer break? Did she say she might stop by to see me?"

Oh, Kevin, you do love her so much...I'm not the one who you need. You need her. But I imagine that she's not planning on coming here. I wish I could help you, but I'm afraid I already did everything I was able to do. Too bad it isn't enough.

Feeling sad and wanting to deflect the conversation, Anna blurted, "Kevin, you're asking me ten questions at a time! Which one should I answer? Slow down."

She paused a second, then continuing with, "I don't know what Ann's doing this summer break, but she went to see Steve after she and I finished our conversation. I hope that talking to me will change things up and Ann'll be talking to her dad again. He sure needs that... and she probably needs it even more." Anna was desperate to shift the conversation to a different, less painful subject.

"That's good. I'm glad to hear that. She was literally broken after her parents divorced. Poor Ann...so...did she say anything about coming back to see me?" This question was clearly the heart of Kevin's earlier questions. Anna saw so much anticipation in his eyes. She hated the thought of squashing his hopes.

"You know, we were so busy talking about this whole thing with both sides and comparing our lives, and talking about Steve…"

"I got it. She is not coming." Kevin interrupted her. His eyes had dulled.

"Kevin…" Anna saw so much pain in his eyes. It was hard to watch him like that.

Can I convince her to come visit him? Should I tell him I'll try? But what if I can't? And does he want to see her if that means begging her?

The silence was uncomfortable again. It was one of those moments where you wanna talk about nonsense, such as the weather and who cares what else, because it just felt so awkward to be silent…

"Will you come again tomorrow?" Kevin was the first one to break the silence. He either sense the discomfort Anna's silence signified, or it was his simple way of indicating that he wanted her to leave so he could be alone with his thoughts.

"Of course, I will. Okay, I will get going now. Have a good night." Anna headed toward the door.

"Good night."

Anna turned around to wave, but his eyes were already closed, shutting out the world and her.

Forty-Five

"Ann…please…can you do this for me?" Anna hated begging, but that's exactly what she was doing. It mattered too much to let pride interfere.

"Anna, please don't! Just don't! What's the point? I can't go see him suffer and feel guilty over breaking up with him all over again.

Things happen in life. People break up, people move one. That's normal. Kevin's cancer wasn't the reason for me to break up with him. I've told you this so many times already. It was just a coincidence. It just happened.

We were kids. We were best friends, and then at one point, it turned into love for Kevin. But not for me, not really. I just couldn't help it. Love happens or it doesn't. You can't force it." Ann's passionate, entreating tone made it seem like she was begging, too—begging for Anna to hear her out, for her alternate self to understand, to let Ann not go see Kevin.

"Ann, I get it. Really. I'm not asking you much at all! I'm not asking you to actually love him. I'm not asking you to pretend that you love him. I'm simply asking you to go see him, talk with him...for the sake of everything you once had, for the sake of your childhood friendship, if for no other reason. You were *best friends*." Anna looked straight into Ann's eyes, hoping that the other girl would not be able to say no.

"Anna...I don't know..."

"Kevin's so much worse than the last time you saw him a month ago. You have to know that. He's getting much weaker. He's almost always sleeping these days, and when he wakes up, what's the first thing he does? He asks me if you had stopped by, if you called, if I talked to you, if I'm going to see you again soon.

And then he goes back to sleep. He's almost not eating these days. The nurse has increased his Morphine drip several times over the past week. I overheard her talking to Elizabeth, and she said he doesn't have much time left, especially with him not eating. Elizabeth was crying in the kitchen, but I was too afraid to go talk to her."

"Stop it. I can't hear this anymore. I can't take it. I can't." Ann's voice was harsh, broken sounding.

Anna was taken aback by the other girl's tone of voice. She had been hoping that she would make Ann agree, but her own words didn't appear to be working. Anna didn't know what to say next, but she didn't want to give up.

"I'll come tonight." Ann said quietly, suddenly.

Anna wasn't sure if she had heard the other girl correctly.

"You mean...?"

"Yes, I will come to visit him tonight. Will you be there?"

"Only if you want me to." Anna wasn't sure what else she could say to that. She was surprised by Ann's sudden agreement to see Kevin. She had been begging Ann for the past month—all without letting Kevin know, but nothing had seemed to work until this sudden and surprising concession.

"Yes, please be there, Anna. You're the one doing everything for him these days. And if my visit will make things worse, I hope you'll have a solution."

"Sure. Should I tell him you're coming?"

"It's up to you. Okay, I gotta go now. I'll see you at Kevin's at seven."

Ann was gone before Anna had a chance to respond.

"Seven it is then," Anna said aloud to herself.

Forty-Six

$\mathcal{A}$nna decided not to tell Kevin anything. She was too nervous that something would happen—that Kevin would get too excited, that he would start asking her if it was really Ann's decision to come see him or if Anna had made her come. But mostly, Anna was nervous that Ann would change her mind and not come.

At a quarter past seven, Anna was still waiting, and while Kevin was sleeping, she considered if she should text Ann to see where she was. But just then, the door to his bedroom opened, and she saw the other girl.

"You came!" she voiced quietly.

"Well, I said I was coming, so I don't know why you're looking so surprised." Ann sounded a little irritated, but kept her voice low also. Anna decided that Ann's tone must just be nerves.

Ann came closer to Kevin's bed, and then both of her hands went to her heart. Anna could tell that it was a reflex movement: Ann was shocked by what she saw. It wasn't the Kevin that she had seen even a month ago when she came to find out why her mom was told that she was seen at the hospital.

Anna came closer as well. She touched Ann's shoulder. She was sure that it wasn't easy for her. She had come to know that

Ann was a good person; she had a good heart, and it didn't matter if she loved Kevin or not. He was dying, and Ann clearly recognized the fact at this moment.

"I didn't think it would be this bad. He's so skinny." Ann whispered as tears were running down her face.

"You want me to leave? Do you wanna have some time alone with him?" asked Anna.

"If you don't mind," whispered Ann.

Anna said nothing further, just squeezed Ann's shoulder and left the room. She was sure that the other two had things to talk about.

Anna was walking on empty streets, lost in her thoughts. On one hand, Anna was so happy that Ann had finally agreed to come see Kevin again. She was sure that it wasn't just him who needed the time together. Ann needed it as well. She needed to see him at least one more time. And the time was coming soon now.

It was obvious even to Anna that Kevin was simply fading away. Morphine was keeping him relaxed and asleep for most of the daylight and night hours. But when it wasn't enough and he was in pain again, the nurse would simply increase the drip rate, and then he would be comfortable and asleep again.

Summer was coming to an end also. The next school year would start shortly. Ann would be going back to school.

As for Anna herself, she simply didn't know. She had no idea what was going to happen to her.

Will I find a way back to my side? Will I be able to start school as well? How much time will pass on the other side by the time I'm back? If I get back...

Will Kevin be happy to see me, or will he not believe my stories again? There were others thoughts as well; Anna was terrified by them. But they kept coming, despite her best efforts to ignore them.

When Kevin dies here, will my Kevin still be all right on the other side? And how will I get back to him?

And that was her biggest question—the one she was afraid to ask even herself. The one she didn't have an answer for.

Suddenly, Anna felt her phone vibrating in her pocket. She pulled the phone out and looked. It was a text message from Ann.

Ty 4 making me visit. I needed that. I did! ...not just Kevin.

Oh Ann Im so glad. U ok? U wanna meet n talk? Anna sent her the reply.

No. But TY. Need some time alone.

Ok. Should I go back 2 him now? Anna wasn't sure what she to do next, and it was getting really late. While she'd been aimlessly walking, it had become pitch dark outside without her really noticing.

I think you should go home. It's late. Kevins sleeping.

But u got a chance 2 talk? Anna was suddenly worrying that Kevin might have slept through the whole thing and wouldn't know that Ann had been there.

Yeah, we talked 4 a while. @ 1st, he didnt even recognize me. thought I was u. But only 4 a second. Ann was a quick texter. Her responses were almost instantaneous.

Ann, ty for not getting mad @ me n 4 going to see him. Sorry, I know I put pressure on u this last month.

Dont be sorry. Im glad u did. Ok, Anna. say hi 2 my dad. Text me tomorrow.

Done texting, Anna continued walking and finally felt peace inside. She felt like she had accomplished something good today. It was a victory, even if a small one. But it was a victory, nonetheless—one that she had won for Kevin. Maybe for Ann as well. Ann had said that she needed the visit, too.

Forty-Seven

The next morning Anna was back by Kevin's side, waiting for him to wake up. She was so excited to hear him talk about Ann, about their visit last night. She couldn't wait to see him smile. She hadn't seen it in a while now.

Anna was getting inpatient. She was fidgeting in the chair, staring down and flipping through his photo album again. Then she heard Kevin moving in the bed. The next second she shifted and was sitting on his bed.

"Good morning. How're you feeling?" Anna asked quietly.

"Ann…you came again. I'm so happy to see you. Missed you. I missed you so much, Ann…" Kevin's voice was hoarse.

Oh no! No, no, no…I'm not Ann! I can't let him think that!

"Kevin…" Anna wasn't sure what to say. She choked back her tears.

"Ann…I love you. I'm so glad…I'm so glad I got a chance to say it again. I was scared yesterday. But today I'm not…Not scared anymore. Because you came back. I love you so much and I always did. I was waiting for you…to come back…and I always knew you'd come back."

Anna was crying. She couldn't talk. She couldn't bring herself to tell him that she wasn't his Ann.

Doesn't he see that it's me? I've been here every single day for the last month! Or is it the Morphine making him confused?

Should I tell him? Should I not? But what's the point? Maybe this is the reason why I'm here? Didn't I come here to make things better for him? And Ann is everything to him.

But is it really okay for me to let him think she's here? How can it be okay?!

While Anna was still trying to decide, Kevin looked at her, his eyes bright, just like they used to be when she had seen him for the first time.

"Ann, you're the best thing that ever happened to me. Please know that. I want you to be happy in life. Please...let yourself be happy. Just know...just know that you made me so happy... please let someone make you that happy one day..."

And in that moment, Anna knew why she was here: She came to make Kevin happy, and he was happy in this moment. The rest simply didn't matter.

"I love you, Kevin...I love you so so much...I always did, and I always will." Then she leaned closer and gently kissed his lips.

For a moment, Kevin kissed her back. Then he closed his eyes and fell immediately back asleep. Morphine was doing its job...

Anna stood up and went outside. She needed the fresh air. She needed to think.

Forty-Eight

When Anna went back to Kevin's house about an hour later, she felt a lot better. She had walked around outside. She pondered more about what had happened, and she finally convinced herself that she had done the right thing. And then she was ready to go back.

Anna knocked on the front door and waited a minute. She knew that Elizabeth was at home, but no one answered. Anna wasn't sure if she should use the key Elizabeth had given her a week ago.

Finally, Anna gave up on waiting. She got the key out from her backpack and was going to open the door for herself, but then the door opened.

Elizabeth was standing in the doorway, just looking at her, not saying anything. But Anna knew in that very moment that it had happened.

Kevin had passed away.

Part 3

Forty-Nine

Anna sat in the coffee shop, staring outside through the window and thinking. It had been almost three months since Kevin passed away, but it still felt like yesterday. Her feelings were as raw as they had been on the day it happened. Anna kept telling herself that time would make everything better—she would feel better soon.

That's what they say, right? All hurts heal in time. I hope.

Anna looked down at the notebook in front of her. She had been working on the same drawing for many days now but still hadn't been able to finish it. The drawing was of Kevin, the way she had seen him that last time when he thought she was Ann. It was his eyes and facial expression that Anna was struggling with. He had gazed at her so differently that time—with such love—because he thought she was Ann.

"Hey, Anna! Sorry I'm late. You been waiting a while?" It was Ann. They had agreed to meet today and, yes, Anna had been waiting for some time. But what else did she have to do?

"Hey, nice to see you. No, don't worry. I have all the time in the world, so it's not a problem."

"I'll go order something to drink. You want anything?" asked Ann.

"No, I'm good. Thanks, though."

Ann came back shortly carrying two iced coffees.

"Here's one for you. You look like you could use some coffee."

"Oh. Thanks." That was all Anna said. She knew exactly how she looked nowadays. She saw herself in the mirror each morning. She appeared tired, exhausted, almost depressed. That's certainly how she felt these days. She also felt trapped. She was trapped. She wanted to go home. She wanted to be with Kevin...with her Kevin.

Anna and Ann both were quiet for a time, considering what to say next.

"Have you talked to your mom lately?" Anna was the first one to break the silence.

"Yeah, I tried a few days ago. Nothing's changed. She threatened me that she will take me to see a mental health specialist if I bring up the conversation about the other side one more time." Ann looked uncomfortable saying that.

"Oh! I'm sorry that I'm causing so much trouble."

"Don't be sorry, Anna! I keep bringing it up because I want my mom to *forgive* dad. I want her to *believe* him. I want her to *accept* him the way I accepted him and you. I want them to be together again. I want to have our family back!" Ann was getting emotional.

"Shhh...It's okay. It will get better. It will. One day she'll understand everything," offered Anna, while not being very convinced of her own words.

"One day might be too late. You know that."

Ann looked terribly sad, and Anna felt that sadness like it was her own. She knew just too well how it was to worry about a parent in your life. She didn't know what to say next.

"I will try again, though. I mean, I will try to come here with my mom again. Still, I'm not sure if I should risk talking to her about the other side again. Knowing her, she will take me to see a crazy doctor, and that's the last thing I need right now. But I'm sure I can set up a coffee shop visit again. Maybe even tomorrow?"

"Ann, we've tried how many times now? Five or six? It's not working. I can't get to the other side when you and your mom are here. It was Kevin who was getting me back home. You were my pathway to come here but not to get back home."

"I know. But we gotta try again! You can't just give up. I know how badly you wanna get home. I know how much you love Kevin. It's obvious. You don't even have to tell me. Let's try again tomorrow. Okay?"

Anna knew that Ann was trying to be helpful. But it didn't matter. She was stuck. She couldn't get home without Kevin being here.

Anna looked outside. She saw yellow and orange leaves drifting down. The image looked gorgeous, but it looked sad at the same time.

Maybe she needed to get used to the idea that she didn't have her own home on the other side any longer. This was her home now. Even if it didn't feel like one.

Fifty

They tried again the next day, just as they had planned. Ann convinced Maria to stop by the coffee shop after Maria picked Ann up from school. Anna had been waiting for them for a few hours while alternating between reading her book and working on her drawing of Kevin. Because what else did she have to do?

Ann and Maria ordered to-go drinks and went outside with Anna following them, but as soon as she stepped outside, she knew that it hadn't worked. Again. She was still on the other side, not at home.

Anna didn't know how many more time she would be willing to try again. Every time caused her increased amounts of stress and anxiety. She was terrified of Maria, which she knew was ridiculous, but she couldn't help it. Anna wasn't even exactly sure why she felt that way about Ann's mother, but she did. Maybe she was scared that Maria would take her to the mental health institution if the woman would notice her. That idea was nonsense, though.

She can't really do that, can she? Anna didn't want to find out.

But most of all, Anna was terrified of things not working out. She wasn't able to get back home to her side, and every time she tried and it failed, she felt even more depressed and scared that it was never going to happen.

Anna saw Maria and Ann get into their SUV and then take off. She stood around the corner, head down, tears in her eyes. She hoped Maria hadn't noticed her standing there.

A minute later her phone was vibrating. Anna knew it was from Ann.

Srry, Anna. I really hoped it'd work this time. Wondering what we're doing wrong. Anna read the text.

I told you so many times whats wrong! Kevin isnt here, that's whats wrong. That was how I got home before. He went 2 the coffee shop w/ me n it just happened. Giving her response, Anna was becoming even more frustrated.

But we have 2 b able 2 do something?!

Anna didn't reply to the latest text message, but her phone was already vibrating again.

R u okay? I hate leaving you like this. U want me 2 come back? We could go 4 a walk in the park.

Anna considered that idea for a moment, but she decided to decline Ann's proposal. She just wanted to be alone. Plus, Anna knew that Ann had homework to do. And she had a life besides babysitting her.

I'm ok. No, I actually have plans 4 2nite. But ty.

Anna contemplated the response she'd just sent, thinking about how stupid the words had sounded even to herself. *Plans for tonight? Really? These words right after I tried getting to the other side?! And suddenly I have plans. You're making the lamest excuses now…*

Let me know if u change ur mind. Call me if u wanna talk.
Anna read the last text message before putting her phone away.

Actually, I do have plans for tonight! Even if I just planned this. I'll go visit Kevin.

Fifty-One

*A*nna was sure that some people would find it strange, but she liked going to the cemetery and spending time there. She didn't think it was creepy or weird at all. She actually felt really peaceful. When she visited, she calmed inside; she could sort through all her thoughts and feelings there, and she could find sense in her life again. There, where there was no more life…

Anna was sitting by Kevin's grave, looking at the little tombstone with his name and birth and death dates on it.

He had such a short life. It's so unfair… What was the reason for him even being in this world? Why're some children born, just to die a few years later? Or days? Why does it happen? How hard it must be for the parents…I wonder if there'll ever be an answer to this question…

"Anna?" Hearing her name suddenly called, her thoughts were interrupted. She was startled. She turned around and saw Elizabeth approaching her.

"Hello. Sorry. I didn't expect anybody here. I'm always alone when I come," said Anna.

"No, I'm the one who's sorry. I didn't mean to scare you. You've come here before?" asked Elizabeth.

"You mean to visit Kevin? Oh yeah, I come at least once a week."

Elizabeth didn't say anything, but Anna could see that the woman was surprised. Then Elizabeth sat down next to Anna, right on the ground without hesitating.

"I come here a lot as well…after work or on my days off. It feels good to spend some time here with him. I feel peaceful here. I like talking to Kevin, too. I tell him about home life, about his sisters, about my work, about everything. Is that strange?"

Anna didn't expect the question, but she replied quickly.

"No, not at all." Then she added, "I talk to him, also. It helps me, you know…"

Elizabeth was quiet for a few moments, and then there was another question that Anna didn't expect.

"Can you tell me about Kevin…from your side, I mean?"

"Um…sure! What do you wanna know?" asked Anna.

"It's up to you. Whatever you want to share with me."

"Let's see…First of all, Kevin is a very nice person. Everyone likes him…at home and at school. And now at work."

"Is he working?"

"Yes, the minute my Kevin turned sixteen, he got a job. That was his goal, so he could help his mom. She works a lot."

"Does she? Anna…What about Kevin's dad? Does he live with them?"

"No…he died of a brain tumor. And that's why Elizabeth is working so much."

"So, it was a brain tumor? Just like it happened here…"

Anna looked at Elizabeth. She wasn't crying, but she looked very sad.

"Yeah, Kevin told me. And that's why I'm so scared!" interjected Anna.

"Scared of what, sweetie?"

"I didn't tell this to anybody. I feel like talking about this can make it happen…But still, I feel like I can tell you."

Elizabeth just looked at Anna with her warm eyes, not urging her to talk but clearly caring.

"If Kevin's dad died on both sides…Does it mean, does it mean that Kevin…" Anna couldn't finish her question.

"Oh, Anna, have you been worried about your Kevin? No, dear, I don't think that's how it works. Kevin's dad was just a coincidence. Look at everything else—it's all pretty different, isn't it? From what you've told me, your and Ann's lives seem very different, despite how you two look alike. Even your relationships with Kevin have been different."

Anna knew what Elizabeth had said must be right. What the woman had said made perfect sense. Anna was so glad that she finally brought up her worst fear and talked to someone, especially such a special someone, Kevin's mom.

"What else is bothering you, Anna? How is life overall? What's your plan? To be here for a while and then go back home? Or are you staying here for good?"

"It's all complicated…my plan was to be here with Kevin until…until the end, you know. I saw him the first time on this side, and then I found out about Ann breaking up with him. I felt like I had to do *something* about it. I felt like I had to make it better for him somehow. So, I came. But it was Kevin who had been getting me back home. Without him, it doesn't seem to work anymore. I can't get back home."

"Oh, Anna…" said Elizabeth softly. Then she gently hugged the girl, and they sat silently like that, both gazing at the little sign with Kevin's name placed in front of them.

"Do you regret doing this?" asked Elizabeth finally.

"No! No, please don't even think that. Honestly, I knew that there was a chance that I'd be coming here for good. But I was hoping something would happen, and I'd be able to come back… maybe it's still possible. Maybe one day something will happen. I don't know. But I definitely don't regret anything I did. It's the best thing that I've ever done in my life."

"You're such a good girl, Anna. I hope you recognize that. And I also hope that you will get home soon. You deserve to go back and be with your Kevin, spend your whole life loving each other."

That's all I want…I wanna spend my life loving him…

Fifty-Two

A few weeks later, Anna was having a serious conversation with Steve. Steve had been very supportive and helpful with everything that was happening. He always took her side; he had agreed with everything Anna wanted to do, until this moment.

"Anna, this can't go on forever. It's time to *do* something with your life."

"Like what?!" Anna realized she was shouting at him.

"First of all, you need to go back to school." Steve remained calm.

"How? I can't go to school here. I'm nobody here! I don't even exist here." Anna was on the edge of tears. She felt so small; she felt so insignificant; she felt so helpless.

"That's exactly what I wanna help you with but you wouldn't let me. It's time to do something. You can't live like this. You do exist, and it's about time to admit it and start acting like it."

"Steve, I get it…but honestly, all I wanna do is to get back home. Even if my life wasn't great there, I was happy in my own way.

Even if I didn't realize it until now, I was someone there! I was Anna! ...Anna who attended school...who was known by other people...who had her own irresponsible mom...who had learned how to take care of herself...Anna who loved Kevin more than she loved anybody else.

And that's the life I wanna get back to. Everything else doesn't matter."

"I know, Anna. I really do. And I want you to get back. I've supported you with everything you've done. And I'll continue to do so. But, at the same time, I can't just stand idly by while you're clearly stuck here. We need to do something."

"Steve, give me some more time. Please. I don't wanna do anything. Not just yet. I wanna try again. And I know Ann will help me with it."

"How many times have you tried?" questioned Steve.

"Nine," answered Anna.

Without saying a word, Steve looked as if his point had been proven. He didn't need to say anything.

Nevertheless, Anna persisted, pleading, "Let me try one more time."

"One more?" confirmed Steve.

"Yes! Just one more time. But not yet. I wanna wait a little bit. Ann is busy with Thanksgiving coming up this week, and then Christmas shopping will be next. I'll wait until after Christmas, and then I will try again...one last time. If it doesn't work, I'll let you help me at that point. I'll finally have to admit that my life is here now. I just need more time to accept this possibility, though, and that one last chance."

"Okay, that sounds fair to me."

Then Steve came closer and gave her a hug. Anna felt like it was exactly what she needed—just a little more support and understanding—on top of what Steve had given her already.

Laying in the bed that evening, Anna was looking at all her pictures on her iPhone. Most of them were of her and Kevin during his last month. It was amazing to Anna how happy he looked in some of them. He looked so happy despite knowing that he was going to die soon. Anna couldn't quite understand that kind of happiness.

After Kevin had passed away, Anna had barely taken any pictures. She had snapped a few with her and Ann, and she had some at the art museum. One day, when she had felt completely lonely and sad, she went back to the museum in an attempt to remember how she had felt on her first day there. She recalled how happy she had been that day. That day, she had believed she would have a lot more time left with Kevin. That day she didn't know how little time she actually had remaining with him…

So, I have until after Christmas? I can try one more time. But, oh God, I know already that it's not going to work with Kevin not being here! Why did I even ask Steve to give me more time? The sooner I accept that I'm stuck here, the sooner I'll be able adjust to my new life. I understand this really, but something inside of me just can't quite accept it, and I don't wanna give up.

What am I hoping for? For a miracle? Maybe…but even if I get back home, what will I find there? How much time will have passed there? A year? Or maybe even more?! Will Kevin be waiting for me? Will he even believe me? What about my mom? So many questions…

*maybe it'll be better for everyone if I just stay here…for everyone…
everyone but me, that is…*

With these unsettling thoughts, Anna fell asleep. She had
thirty-seven days until Christmas, thirty-seven days to change or
to accept her future, whatever might happen.

Fifty-Three

Christmas was coming. Everyone was counting down the days. Everyone was waiting for the holiday—days off work, family time, and gifts. Anna could feel it in the air. She didn't share the same holiday spirit, though. She wasn't ready for this Christmas, not at all.

Instead, Anna was waiting anxiously to try getting home once again. She and Ann had everything planned. The day after Christmas, Ann and Maria would come to the coffee shop, and Anna would be waiting for them. This time she would grab the door while both Ann and Maria were touching it. She could do this. It could work. Both Anna and Ann had spent hours talking about the detail, and they had even practiced. Anna had her outfit ready for that day. She would look completely different so that Maria would not notice her.

Despite everything being planned out to the smallest detail, Anna felt anxious. *What if it doesn't work?*

And deep inside, Anna knew that the plan would not, could not work. It just wouldn't. Grabbing the door while Ann and Maria touched it would not help—because it wasn't them who had gotten her home in the past. It was Kevin. It had always been him.

Anna knew that she needed a miracle in order to get home. But she didn't really believe in miracles. So, while planning it all, Anna was also planning an alternative life. The one she would have once this last and final attempt failed.

I will need to start school here. But I can't go to the school Ann is going to. That would be too confusing and lead to too many questions. It also means that I won't know anyone at my new school. I will be a stranger. I will be so lonely…it's okay, though. I can make new friends. I will manage.

I will have to talk to Steve pretty soon here. I still don't know his plan. He said he could help me to become a legal person on this side. I'll need some kind of documents to go to school, right? …Like an ID or something. That I don't know, but I'm sure Steve will manage.

And now I'll be turning sixteen in less than a week…that means I can finally work. I need to find a job but, again, I will need documents, I'm sure. Yeah, I definitely can't live much longer like this. Steve is right. Plus, I can't let him have me here and be supporting me any longer. I need to get a job.

Later that day, Anna decided to go to the store. The Christmas Spirit seemed to be contagious after all. She wanted to buy gifts for Steve and Ann—and maybe even one for Elizabeth. Anna didn't have a lot of money, just some cash that she had saved from the pocket money that Steve had been giving her over the last few months. She thought that it should be enough to buy three small gifts, nevertheless. To Anna, gifts didn't have to be expensive; they just had to be meaningful.

Shopping brought Anna's mood up. She felt much better walking home that evening, carrying three gifts in a paper bag. She bought a small notebook for Ann. It was decorated with two small owls, and there was a caption below the picture: "You are always in my heart." Anna and Ann had become really close over the summer and fall. Ann had become like a sister to her. Ann was the sister that Anna had never had.

There was a t-shirt for Steve. It was green, his favorite color. It said "#strong" on the front and, to Anna, that word represented everything Steve was. He was one mentally strong person. He had lost his family; his own daughter had stopped talking to him, but he still found the strength to help Anna with everything that was happening in her crazy and complicated life. Anna never felt like she was a burden to him when he helped her; Steve always made her feel welcomed and even loved.

And there was a bracelet for Elizabeth in Anna's bag, too. It was very simple, but Anna hoped that Elizabeth would like it. The bracelet was a single string of light pink pearls with one gold colored pearl in the strand. There was one single word on that pearl, "mom." Anna thought for a long time before she decided to buy the bracelet. She wondered if such gift was appropriate since she wasn't Elizabeth's daughter. But after considering for a while, Anna decided to go with it.

Elizabeth was a great mom, both on Anna's own side and on this side. She was everything a child needed—caring, loving, understanding, fun, enthusiastic, smart, and hard working. Anna just hoped that Elizabeth would understand why she had chosen this gift for her.

Anna was counting down the days. She was excited to give her gifts to people that she loved. Maybe she was even starting to accept her new life on this side?

Whatever the case, there were only two more days left until Christmas.

Fifty-Four

It was Christmas Eve, and Anna decided not to wait on giving her gifts any longer. First, she went to see Elizabeth. Once she neared the woman's house, though, Anna felt nervous. She hadn't been there since the day of Kevin's funeral. Anna felt like it had been a long time ago. But suddenly, all the emotions and feelings were flooding through her all over again. After she finally felt that she had learned to keep them deep inside.

Kevin, oh Kevin, I miss you so much. I need you in my life. Why? Why did it have to be you and not someone else? Someone who wasn't as kind or someone who didn't love life the way that you did? Someone who wasn't part of my life…why?

Anna stood in front on the house, weeping, not able to calm herself. Minutes passed by, and she was getting cold. Finally, Anna decided that it was okay to feel sad. Kevin was gone, and she couldn't deny it. She couldn't deny her feelings either; they were real and Elizabeth would understand, more than anyone.

With tears still in her eyes and on her cheeks, Anna knocked on the door. She waited for a few seconds and then knocked again, louder this time.

The door opened, and Anna saw Elizabeth. The woman looked like she had just been crying as well. Anna wondered if she had been.

"Anna? Come on in, sweetheart. It's very nice to see you."

"I'm sorry I didn't call ahead. I wasn't even sure if you'd be home. I won't take a lot of your time."

"Oh, that's okay, Anna! I'm just glad you came. Follow me to the kitchen. I don't wanna burn the dinner."

Anna followed Elizabeth to the kitchen. Then she sat down in one of the chairs, and immediately there was a mug of hot chocolate placed in front of her. That's how Elizabeth was, always welcoming and caring.

She's the same on both sides…

"So, how have you been, hon?" asked Elizabeth.

"I'm okay, finally getting used to things. I'm thinking about going back to school after Christmas break."

"Oh Anna…" There was both sadness and understanding in Elizabeth's eyes. She knew that staying wasn't Anna's choice. Anna was simply stuck here.

"It's okay. I'll get used to it." Anna sounded more confident than she actually felt. But it was Christmas Eve after all, and she hadn't come to ruin Elizabeth's holiday and mood with her own problems.

"Please, come visit me more often," pleaded Elizabeth. Then she added quietly, "…if you end up staying here."

"I will," responded Anna. Then the girl took another sip of her hot chocolate. It was delicious.

"I came because I wanted to wish you a Merry Christmas. And I brought you a little gift." Anna took a tiny box out from her backpack; it was covered in gold and red wrapping paper that she had found at Steve's house.

Anna handed the gift to Elizabeth, adding, "Thank you for everything you've done for me."

Elizabeth had tears in her eyes again. Anna could tell that she was very emotional. Elizabeth didn't say anything. Instead, she came around and hugged the girl tightly. She held Anna like that for a long time.

"It's the other way around, you know. It's me who has to thank you. You don't realize what you did for my son. You probably don't even realize just how much he loved you."

"Ann. He loved Ann." Anna couldn't help it; she had to correct Elizabeth.

"You're right. He loved Ann. But Kevin on your side loves you, too. To me, it's all the same. It's just different versions of us. And at the very end, Kevin thought you were Ann.

I know that, Anna. I was in the doorway when he was talking to you that day. You didn't see me. But I had come to check on him. Then I left to give you privacy.

What you've done shows the kind of person you are. Not everyone would do that. You left your own home to come help him in his final days, and you haven't even taken credit for it! You let him think you were Ann, and that decision made his final hours happy. I know he was happy…" Elizabeth couldn't talk after the last statement. She was in tears, sobbing in Anna's arms.

Anna held her, letting Elizabeth cry her heart and sorrow out. Anna felt that today Elizabeth needed just that—someone to listen and comfort her.

And after, Anna left the house wondering if she would ever see Elizabeth again. *What if it actually works this time?*

Then Anna went to see Ann.

Talking to the other girl was a lot easier. Things didn't get so emotional. Anna simply gave Ann the gift, but then Ann needed to go back inside before Maria could start wondering who she was seeing outside so late in the evening.

"Thanks for coming, Anna, and thanks for the gift. I love it. It's so you. It's a good thing I like owls, too." Ann was laughing as she offered those words.

"Okay, you should go back inside. It's too cold outside, and you're shivering. Text me tomorrow with the exact time you're going to be at the coffee shop so that I can come early."

"Okay. I think I'll be there around three o'clock, but I'll make sure to text you tomorrow."

"Sounds good," Anna said, turning around to leave. But Ann was talking to her again.

"Anna! I'll have your gift when I come to the coffee shop. I can't go in the house now to get it. Mom would start asking questions," stated Ann.

"No worries." Anna simply smiled at the other girl and waved goodbye as she was walking away.

Just as Anna reached Steve's house, she realized what had been bugging her on the walk there.

Ann'll have a gift for me when she comes to the coffee shop. But we aren't going to be talking there! She can't even show that she knows me because Maria will be there.

So, does that mean Ann's so sure it's not going to work? Is she completely certain that our plan is going to fail again?

Or was she not thinking about it at all when she said she'd be bringing me a gift?

I really wanna know what she's thinking even though it's not going to change anything. Things will happen the way they're going to happen despite what Ann or I think. It's about time for me to accept life the way it's going to be...

When Anna got into the house, she was surprised that Steve wasn't there yet. That was unusual. He rarely worked late in the evenings, especially not on holidays. She decided to call just to make sure he was okay. She dialed his number, but there was no answer. That made Anna worry a little bit.

What if something's happened? What if he's gotten into a car accident?

While Anna was still considering the terrible possibilities, her phone vibrated in her hand. It was a text message from Steve.

Sorry, got totally slammed at work. Didn't get a chance to call you. And sorry to leave you at home alone on Christmas Eve. But we'll do something fun tomorrow. We'll see if Ann can join us too.

Anna texted him back. *It's okay, I'm fine. Just was worried about u. Coming home soon?*

Anna waited a moment for his longer response, then read it.

I'm afraid it's going to be a few more hours, kiddo. Just bake yourself a pizza or order some food, don't go hungry all evening. Okay? And there's a new movie on the coffee table. I thought we'd watch it together. But just go ahead and watch it tonight if you want to.

Ok, ty. Dont worry about me. I'm fine. C u soon! Anna texted while thinking once again just how caring Steve was.

Perfect dad...just not really mine...

Anna opened the freezer, took the frozen pizza out, looked at the baking instructions, and then she put it back. She didn't want pizza.

Then Anna went to the coffee table and looked at the movie. The description looked like it would be a fun comedy, but she put it down as well. She didn't want to watch anything.

Instead, Anna walked to the front entryway. She quickly pulled her coat and her hat on and went outside.

Anna was going to the coffee shop. Never mind that it would be empty on Christmas Eve. Never mind that the shop would be closing in less than an hour. She just wanted to go there, sit behind the table in her favorite corner, and sort her thoughts and feelings out.

As Anna was walking toward the coffee shop, however, she suddenly remembered her gift for Steve. She had completely forgotten and left it out on the couch in the living room along with the card that she had signed for him. She didn't want Steve to see it because she wanted to give it to him herself.

It's okay. I'll probably be home before him anyway.

Anna hadn't realized how cold it had gotten outside in the time after she had come back from visiting Elizabeth and Ann. But it was getting colder and colder with each step that she took.

That's okay. I'm just a few minutes away.

And then it started snowing.

Fifty-Five

Anna was sitting in her favorite spot. Her table in the corner wasn't always available on this side like it was at home, but today, on Christmas Eve, the coffee shop was completely empty. There was one young couple who had stopped by briefly to grab to-go drinks, but that was it.

The barista kept disappearing periodically into the room behind the counter as well. But Anna was okay with that. Today, she just wanted to be alone; she didn't want any company. The deserted shop and her corner in particular was a perfect atmosphere for thinking.

Anna got out her notebook from the backpack and opened to the page where she was still working on the drawing of Kevin. Without focusing too much on her pencil, she started drawing, completely lost in her thoughts.

Anna was contemplating the day that she had gotten to this side. It had been the beginning of summer, but now it was Christmas already. That day, she had no idea that she would stay here for quite so long. She had thought about it, of course she had; she had even faintly considered the possibility back then.

Anna realized now, though, that she had been naïve in hoping for something just to happen. That was it – she was just naïve. She had been hoping deep inside that Kevin would somehow get all better, hoping that she would make Ann come back to him, hoping that she would get home after a happy ending.

But the ending hadn't been happy. Ann never went back to Kevin; she even said that she hadn't loved him…and Kevin never got better and passed away from leukemia…and Anna was still here on the other side. She was still waiting for something to happen…

Before Anna even realized it, her drawing was finished. She had finally completed it! On the page, Kevin was captured just as he had looked that day—looking at her with such love in his eyes, thinking that Anna was his Ann.

Anna leaned back in her chair and stared at the drawing some more. She liked it a lot. She even thought that it might just be her best drawing ever. But maybe it wasn't, and Anna was just imagining it because she loved everything that had anything to do with Kevin.

Kevin. I always think about him. It doesn't even matter what I'm doing or what I'm thinking about…I end up thinking about Kevin anyway. It's like my whole life is circling around him! How will I ever manage if I end up being stuck here forever without him?!

That last thought terrified Anna, but she didn't have an answer to the question. Not yet anyway. Maybe one day she would learn to move on and live without him. Or not…

Wanting a break from her dark contemplations, Anna stood up and went to look through the window. It was beautiful outside.

It had continued to snow since she had come to the coffee shop, and now everything looked white and sparkly.

Still snowing. So beautiful. White Christmas. It looks amazing. So peaceful and quiet with everyone else in their homes and the streets empty and dark. It's magical…

Anna wanted to be a part of the magic. She walked back to her table, grabbed her backpack and her coat, and went outside.

Once Anna stepped out the door, she felt the freezing cold, but it didn't matter. She felt an indescribable magic in the air, and it was truly amazing. Anna took a deep breath and the frigid air filled her lungs. Wanting to enjoy the moment as much as possible, Anna decided to walk home slowly. She ignored the cold.

After Anna took a few steps, though, she suddenly remembered her drawing. *Did I pick it from the table, or did I forget it?*

Anna had been so preoccupied with the magic of a white Christmas that she had completely forgotten the drawing. She quickly checked her backpack. It wasn't there, so she walked back to the coffee shop to get it.

Anna watched her feet as she was stepping in the snow. There was no one else around, so she was the only one leaving footsteps in the white drifts. She thought the snow looked beautiful.

Once back in front of the coffee shop, Anna opened the door and stepped in.

Wow, it's really hot in here, was her immediate thought.

Then Anna looked around, and she couldn't believe her eyes. She wasn't the only person in the shop. There were other people. And they all were wearing dresses, shorts, and sandals.

White Christmas. Magical evening. Oh my God!

As the thoughts ran through her head, Anna was afraid to move. She was afraid to breathe. She was afraid it all would go away. She was afraid that it was just her imagination playing tricks on her.

She continued to stand where she stood, staring in disbelief at everything around her, her thoughts chaotic.

I am home. It happened. It finally happened! But how did it happen?

And then Anna saw him. He was sitting with his back toward her, but Anna recognized his profile immediately. She would always know him. She would always recognize him among thousands of people. He was here. So close…

"Kevin?" Anna heard herself say his name in a low tone.

He turned around right away and now was looking directly at her. There was clear disbelief in his eyes.

Kevin looks so different. What's happened to his hair? What about those glasses? He never wore glasses before. And a white button-down shirt? Kevin hates those kinds of shirts!

Kevin stood up and walked closer, still silent. Then he lifted his hand up hesitantly and touched Anna's face.

Oh God, that feels so good…I've been dying to feel his touch for months!

"Anna? Is that really you?" Kevin's voice was hoarse.

"Yes, Kevin, it's me! I'm so very happy to see you! These have been the hardest seven months of my life! I wasn't sure if I ever would see you again, and it was just killing me! I'm so happy to be home. I'm so happy to be with you again!" Tears began filling up Anna's eyes, and then she was crying and ineffectively trying to wipe her own face with her hands. The emotions were overwhelming.

"Anna, you look the same…just like the last time I saw you. You still look like a kid." Kevin was still standing in front of her, still staring at her but not touching her face anymore.

Anna didn't know what to say. She was fifteen, yes. She would be turning sixteen in a few days. She was only a few months younger than him, just like she always had been. She didn't understand his comment.

And then it hit her—Anna remembered the time difference. There was a time difference each and every time she had gone to the other side. Anna was afraid to ask. She was more than afraid; she was terrified. But she had to know.

"Kevin. How much time's passed since I left? That day, I mean—the one when I wrote you the letter and left it with your boss at the pizzeria." Anna wasn't sure if she was ready to hear the answer.

Kevin didn't answer right away. He was silent for a moment; then he took his wallet out from his pants pocket. Like magic, he retrieved a piece of paper. He was holding that paper, looking down at it.

Anna recognized what it was immediately. It was the letter she had written that day. Kevin had kept it in his wallet.

Does that mean he always had it with him? What else does it mean? He's been waiting for me to come back?

"Anna, it's been six years and two months since you left… since you wrote this letter." Anna wasn't sure if she heard him correctly. It didn't seem possible.

Six years and two months? Maybe sixteen months? Maybe two years at the most? That I could almost understand. But not six years! No! Kevin is twenty-two? And I'm still not even sixteen? That just can't be right!

"Kevin, honey, I'm back."

Anna heard the strange female voice. It sounded like background noise to Anna's overwhelmed brain. She was in shock, trying to make sense of everything that had happened, everything that she'd just heard.

"Oh, Emily, come over here," Kevin said, paused, then sped up his next words. "This is Anna. Remember I told you about my childhood friend Anna who disappeared years ago, and everyone was looking for her for months and months? This is her. She's back. She's safe. We just ran into each other. A funny thing is that it happened here, at our coffee shop. We used to call it ours because of just how much time we used to spent together here."

Kevin was talking fast—too fast for Anna to catch everything that he was saying or process what it all meant.

And all she could see and focus on in front of her was Emily's huge belly anyway. And Kevin's hand on her shoulder. The rest didn't matter.

"Hi, Anna. I'm Emily, Kevin's wife. I'm so glad you're safe! Kevin talks frequently about you, and now here you are, safe and sound and good looking! You look really good for your age!" Emily was bubbling away, and Anna found it difficult to listen to her.

Kevin's wife…Kevin's wife…Kevin's wife! The words resounded, echoed in Anna's poor head.

It was all Anna could concentrate on. That, and Emily's obviously pregnant belly.

Then Kevin started asking questions. Anna tried to answer, but she knew that she sounded ridiculous and didn't make a lot of sense.

And then Kevin invited her to come visit him and Emily to "talk about the good old times." Anna blurted something out, and then she simply turned around, and left. She opened the front door of the coffee shop and stepped outside.

Anna hoped to see snow, hoped to see a magical white Christmas, hoped to run to Steve's house and forget about what she had just seen and heard. She hoped to escape, get back to the other side, and stay there forever.

But when Anna stepped outside, it wasn't snowing. Instead, the weather was hot and humid. It was hard to breathe. She felt like her lungs were on fire. She started running anyway.

Anna didn't know where she was running to or what exactly she was running from. She didn't know what was waiting for her or what her future would bring at her next. Anna didn't know if her mom was still around, and if she was, if she was still living in the same place. Anna didn't know how to explain her six-year disappearance and still look and sound sane to anyone.

There was so much that Anna didn't know right then. But she did know one thing in her heart—that seeing Kevin happy at his final days had been worth everything she had gone through and everything that she still would have to face. Love meant being willing to sacrifice, no matter what the cost.

And if Anna had a choice, she would do it all over again.

Epilogue

Anna was sitting at her favorite table in the corner—at her favorite coffee shop. It was still her favorite place despite everything that had happened to her here. Because of the coffee shop, her life had taken a dramatic turn, and everything changed at once. But that was Anna's past, a past that she would never want to change.

Customers came and went. Some sat for a time with their books or laptops out. Anna just sipped her latte and observed.

Anna loved watching people. The old man at the opposite corner was busy reading the newspaper; his hair looked very messy. He had lots of hair for someone his obviously senior age. His hands trembled just a little bit. That observation made Anna sad. Old age wasn't a friendly visitor…but then Anna thought how this old man was actually lucky. He got to live so many years— had clearly lived a long life. It was so many more than Kevin was given.

Then Anna turned her attention to a young mom with a toddler. The toddler was laughing joyfully, and the mom was smiling back down at him. The mom was wearing a nice green hat. It was nice looking, Anna thought to herself.

Anna looked outside next. It was only snowing lightly, but more snow was expected later that evening. Anna found it interesting. She hadn't seen another white Christmas since that pivotal time. And now it was snowing again on Christmas Eve. That fact made her smile.

Anna couldn't help it. She started thinking back on that day, the memories flooding her senses. She remembered instantly her feelings when she first saw Kevin again. And Emily. The shock, the disbelief, the desire to go back to the other side.

It was five years ago now, though, and Anna was still here, on this side. Kevin's son must be four years old now, almost five. The funny thing was, Anna and that little boy almost shared birthdays. Anna would be turning twenty-one soon. Technically, she should be older, but she wasn't because of the time she had spent on the other side. She would always just look young for the age her ID claimed.

I'm almost twenty-one...almost old enough to drink legally. The errant thought made Anna smile. She didn't drink and wasn't planning to. She was focused on her education and of course, on her work.

Anna needed to work a lot in order to make her education and living possible. Her life wasn't easy, but she wasn't complaining. At least she was alive. Not like Kevin.

Five years had passed, but Anna felt like nothing had really changed. All her thoughts and feelings were still about Kevin. And it didn't matter how busy and tired she was with school and work, she still thought about him all the time.

Anna needed to head to work, she knew, but instead, she was still sitting at the coffee shop, wondering how quickly she could get there and how many extra minutes she could spend here.

Anna didn't want to leave. She was still hoping, in her innermost heart, for a miracle to happen—like it had done five years ago when they had that last white Christmas. Maybe the miracle hadn't come without a high cost, but Anna didn't discount that the whole experience had been miraculous. And even though Anna wasn't a kid anymore, she still believed in miracles.

Minutes ticked away, and Anna knew that it really was time to go. So, she got up and tossed away her empty cup. Then she grabbed her purse and walked reluctantly toward the door.

Once outside, Anna took a deep breath in and felt the cold air fill up her lungs. It felt good.

Anna started walking away but then she turned around and looked back at the coffee shop again. Then she looked closer. She wasn't sure if she was seeing correctly, so she walked back and came up close to the window. Yes, she had seen it right.

The three of them were sitting at the table, drinking their coffees and chatting. They all looked happy, like a family—Ann, Maria, and Steve. And they looked just the same as she had always remembered them.

Ann still looked like a teenager. She had dyed her hair, and it looked very cute on her. Anna noticed that Maria and Steve were holding hands, and there was a big diamond on Maria's finger. That observation made Anna smile. She couldn't be completely sure, but it looked like Ann's parents were back together again. Moreover, it looked like they were in love.

Anna stood there for another moment or two, and then she turned resolutely around and started walking. Her Christmas miracle had happened.

Made in the USA
Columbia, SC
27 February 2019